Turn Up for Real

THE **SHARP** SISTERS

#3
Turn Up for Real

STEPHANIE PERRY MOORE

darby creek
MINNEAPOLIS

Darby Creek
A division of Lerner Publishing Group, Inc.
241 First Avenue North
Minneapolis, MN 55401 USA

For reading levels and more information, look up this title at
www.lernerbooks.com.

The images in this book are used with the permission of: front
cover: © R. Gino Santa Maria/Dreamstime.com; © SeanPavonePhoto/
Shutterstock.com (background).

Main body text set in Janson Text LT Std 12/17.5.
Typeface provided by Linotype AG.

Library of Congress Cataloging-in-Publication Data

Moore, Stephanie Perry.
    Turn up for real / by Stephanie Perry Moore.
        pages cm — (The Sharp sisters)
    Summary: Sixteen-year-old Slade dreams of being a singing
sensation but as the middle daughter of a mayoral candidate and
a habitual loner she faces many challenges as she learns just how
difficult surviving as an artist can be.
    ISBN 978-1-4677-3726-5 (lib. bdg. : alk. paper)
    ISBN 978-1-4677-4659-5 (eBook)
    [1. Singing—Fiction. 2. Conduct of life—Fiction. 3. Sisters—Fiction.
4. Family life—Fiction. 5. African Americans—Fiction. 6. Christian life—
Fiction.] I. Title.
PZ7.M788125Tur 2014
[Fic]—dc23   2013044040

Manufactured in the United States of America
1 – SB – 7/15/14

In Memory of
Whitney Houston

You songbird, you … your lovely voice
blessed me.
Thank you for living a life with passion,
purpose, and soul.
I love how you pursued your dream at
a young age and
turnt up for real with your first hit,
"Saving All My Love For You."
May all who read this series be as
relentless as you were.

You left a legacy of inspiration in
your music. Now heaven is richer…
miss you!

CHAPTER ONE
SECLUDED

My hips were swaying from the left to the right, poppin' to the beat. My breasts perked up as the spotlight shined down on me. I started making love to the audience as I sang my first few notes. The crowd went wild. I was on stage. I was in my element. My dance moves were on point, and my melody was stellar.

"Slade! Slade! Slade! Slade! Slade!" I was hype until my eldest sister, Shelby, punched me, waking me from my dream.

"Slade, what's wrong with you? We're about to sing happy birthday to Ansli, and you're in your room dreaming again? Come on, girl! It's not always just about you," Shelby shouted.

It was never about me in the Sharp household. Yes, I had my own room and my own space, but I had to share a bathroom with my two sisters who were a grade younger than me. I was salty because my two sisters who were only a grade older than me shared a bathroom between their rooms, and it was much larger than the one the other three of us had to share.

"You didn't have to punch me," I said to her.

Giving me a huff, she said, "Well, we've been calling you forever."

"Forever? Really, Shelby?" I said, frustrated with my big sis.

Shelby loved to exaggerate. Don't get me wrong, I was happy that my family was finally gelling again. Over the last month, our world was turned upside down when Ansli found out that her father shot her mother and then took his own life. She originally thought her biological parents were killed in a car crash. There are five sisters. Three of us were biologically connected—me; Shelby, my older sister; and

Sloan, my younger sister. Ansli, who was the same age as Shelby, and Yuri, who was the same age as Sloan, were biological sisters that my parents adopted.

For years our parents didn't tell Ansli and Yuri that crucial fact. When Ansli found out, she was livid. I think she now understood that Mom and Dad were doing the best they could. They were already young parents with three children, and then they had five. Ansli thought she wanted to live with her maternal grandparents who lived England, which is a place she'd never been to. But once they finally came to visit—and who knows how much those tickets cost—she now knew this was home. I could have told her that. I could have saved them all that money, and they could've helped me cut a demo for my record, so excuse me if I wasn't all excited with the family bonding.

"There you are," my mom said as soon as I came into the family room.

It wasn't like I was missed. Everybody in the house was paired up with someone. Shelby and Ansli were best friends. Sloan and Yuri were too, and then that left me. My mom and dad had each other, and Ansli and Yuri's grand–parents had each other. My older sisters' boyfriends were at the house earlier, but they were both gone now.

I didn't understand why they always wanted me to be a part of the family. I always felt left out. Nobody could get that. However, when it was time for entertainment, they called on good ole' Slade.

"Lead us off in happy birthday!" Sloan demanded, bossing me around like she was older than me. But because I loved to sing anywhere, any place, any time, I began, and everyone joined in.

"You sing so beautifully," Ansli and Yuri's grandmother came up to me and said after we finished.

"Thank you. It's the only thing in this world that I want to do."

"But she needs to get a real dream," my mom piped in.

"Well, I sang in the opera," their grandmother, Mrs. Sanford, stated proudly.

I guess that shocked my mom. She stopped ragging on me then. Ansli's grandmother basically was saying, "Go for yours, young lady," and that's exactly what I intended to do.

My parents were attorneys—smart people with a very lucrative bodily injury practice. "If you get in an accident, insurance companies want to cut your money? Call on Sharp and Sharp, and make sure you're not cut out of a thing" was their commercial. I could hear it playing over and over again in my mind. I so wanted to sing a jingle for them, but they weren't hearing it. I knew I would have to create something, play it for them, and then they *might* let me perform it. However, I didn't have the personal funds to do that. Every dime I got came from my parents.

We lived in a gorgeous, three-story, brick house. With seven thousand square feet we had plenty of space. The five bedrooms that we girls slept in were upstairs. My parents had their master bedroom on the main floor with a guest bedroom across the hall and off the kitchen. The guest bedroom was where Ansli and Yuri's grandparents were staying. Knowing that all the activity was upstairs, I went down to the basement.

I couldn't hang out with my sisters. Shelby and Ansli were all excited to talk about their boyfriends. Who knew what Sloan and Yuri were talking about, and I didn't really care. I just needed to chill. When I went downstairs to turn on BET, MTV, or VH1, I wanted to be inspired. The TV was on a premium movie channel, and my eyes locked in on a naked guy and girl doing some things that I had never seen before in a bed. I couldn't seem to change the channel. I was appalled, but intrigued. Something inside of me that had never been stirred before got all wet and gooey. The lady was on top, then on the bottom. What was going on with me? I'd never been interested in this kind of stuff before, but I was frozen in front of the TV.

"Oh my gosh! Slade, what are you watching?" Yuri yelled out.

I turned, and my eyes widened at the sight of my two younger siblings. I felt dirty.

"You're a nasty heifer," my sister Sloan called out.

"It was on here. It's not like I turned it to this," I tried explaining.

"But it's not like you turned it off either," Sloan quickly challenged. "You need to get somewhere and pray."

Quickly, I got up and turned off the TV. I tried to go upstairs, but Sloan blocked my view. Yuri touched my shoulder. They were ticking me off.

Yuri said, "Are you going through some sort of crisis? Ansli just went through one. Maybe you need to talk to Mom."

Huffing, I grunted, "I don't need to talk to anybody, and you don't need to say anything either, okay? Is life ending? Am I going to hell?"

"Maybe!" Sloan yelled out.

"Ughh! You first, chick," I retorted.

I was so frustrated at them, at myself, and, if I was being honest, at the fact that I didn't get to see the end. What was going on with Slade Sharp? Usually I could tell anyone anything about me, but at that moment, I was far from having it all together. My world was not crystal clear. I wanted to be a singer, but it didn't seem like that would ever happen. Also, I wanted to feel good, and I had no idea where that came from. So many crazy emotions. I just ran all the way upstairs to the bathroom and took a hot shower. It probably needed to be cold, but whatever.

**

"So you guys going to my pageant or what?" I said the next morning to all of my sisters, who were sprawled out in the basement living area like they had a party and didn't invite me.

Granted, the pageant wasn't supposed to start for another four hours, but I had to be there early. Usually when someone in our family had something big going on all of us got excited, all of us supported, and all of us made a big deal out of it. This wasn't just some random talent show I was entering. This was the big Miss Teen Charlotte Pageant.

"What time does the thing start?" Sloan said in a voice that was hardly interested in going.

I answered, "One."

Sloan vented, "Well, it's morning. Bye!"

All of them were growling like they were bears ready to hibernate for the winter, so I just said forget it and went upstairs to pack up to leave. I had a sour face, but as soon as I opened the door to my bedroom, there was my mom holding up a garment bag.

"My baby girl's gonna be so cute today! I had to get you this number." She unzipped the garment bag, and the sparkly, strapless, silver gown was stunning.

"I didn't think you were going to get me a new one," I said as my eyes teared up. "I honestly didn't think anyone cared."

"I know we've got a lot going on around here. I know we've had one crazy thing after another, particularly with this election, but Slade, I hear you. You told me a few weeks ago that you needed a new evening gown, and you didn't want to recycle what your sister wore to the prom last year. Let's be clear, though. You're a junior. You're wearing this new number to the prom this year."

"Okay, Mom! No problem!" I said in a truly happy tone.

"I'll be ready to take you in about fifteen minutes. When it's over, you can ride home with us. Knowing your dad, there's probably going to be some event that we're going to have to attend. I can't believe we're a month away from the election!"

"He's going to win, Mom," I said, reassuring her.

She wrapped an arm around me and squeezed as if I was cold. "I've got a feeling he's going to win too. And Slade, if you think we're under the microscope now, well it's going to be magnified if he is mayor. Until he actually wins, I'm just taking it day by day. With elections, things get nasty, and who knows what somebody will do to derail his bid."

"Yeah, but who's going to win if he doesn't? Mr. Brown, the Republican? Everyone's talking about how he's a womanizer and doesn't have a chance."

My mom looked at me like I shouldn't say such things, but it was the truth. My birthday was at the end of the month on Halloween, and I'd be seventeen years old. She needed to stop trying to shield me from stuff.

"And then the other guy who's the independent, does he even have a following?" I asked, showing my mom I wasn't just a cute face.

"He's gaining momentum. A lot of the Republicans are putting their support behind him, but don't worry about any of this political stuff. You just get pretty, princess. You're going to win tonight!"

I loved how she supported me. She made me feel like I could do anything. She was always pumping me up—well, except she didn't think singing was a real dream.

***

Thirty minutes later, my confidence waned. When I arrived at the historic Renaissance Theater, there were twenty-three other girls competing for the crown already there. Twenty-four of us total—the largest number of contestants that this pageant has had in a while. We'd been practicing over the past few months, but this was the big day. I kept to myself. That was just my M.O. With everything going on in my family, I felt more comfortable making sure that people liked me for me and not for whose daughter I was.

It wasn't just a pageant. We'd actually been going through different classes to refine us. We had a modeling workshop, an etiquette session, a public speaking workshop, and a fashion do's and don'ts time. In addition, we'd been doing public service projects. We spent time at the old folk's home and with little kids at nursery schools.

I thought I had the pageant on lock. The problem was that we weren't able to see each other's talent, but when we were at the old folk's home last week, another contestant, Miss-Prim-and-Prissy Charlotte Ray, struck a chord. I was blown away when I heard her sing so great for them and had been trying ever since to step up my game. Now that it was the day of the show, it was time to compete, to show what I was made of, and to be ready to give it my all, but my vocal cords were acting up.

"Oh my gosh, I can't compete," I said, pacing back and forth.

I didn't even realize Charlotte was listening. "I got a tea bag, and in this lunch pail is an emergency kit," she said. "Honey, a dab of apple cider vinegar, and some cinnamon. Go put all of this in some hot water, and you'll be fine. If that doesn't work, we can always pray."

"You'd pray for me?" I asked her, feeling bad that I'd been so jealous of her.

"Yeah. You're the stiffest competition in this thing. If you don't compete, I won't get any props if I win. And if I don't win, I'd certainly want the winner to be you. I've heard you sing. You're phenomenal."

"I'm phenomenal?" I said to her, still in disbelief. "You're amazing."

"Yeah, but I can't answer the questions like you can. It's like I know what I want to say. My dad's been interviewing me around the house, I should be good at it by now. He's the superintendent of the schools, for goodness sake, and that's all he's been doing is grilling me, but I still can't seem to nail the questions.

I think that's going to get me today."

"Your dad's the superintendent of schools for Charlotte city schools?"

"Yeah."

"I didn't know because I was in private school, but now I'm at Marks."

"That's where I go. Everybody who is anybody is a Maverick," Charlotte said.

"I haven't seen you around," I said.

"We've only been at school for two months. I think I've seen you or a girl who looks like you. I don't know."

"That was probably one of my sisters."

"Oh, I wish I had sisters. I have two brothers. One older and one younger. Having sisters would be heaven."

"Stick with the brothers. A ton of sisters is drama."

"You're funny," she said to me. "Isn't it crazy? We've been in the same place for some months now, and we've never talked. Most of the girls here paired up. I've seen you alone sometimes, and I wanted to come over and say something to you, but I know how pageants and stuff can be, so I tried once and you looked away. I guess I just felt like you didn't want to be bothered, but is it bad that I'm glad your throat was trippin'?" Charlotte asked.

"Yes. That's the opposite of you saying you wish I was okay. That's what you said a few minutes ago, but I didn't think it was real because this is a competition," I said, truly skeptical and needing her to explain.

"No, I meant that, but I'm saying if your throat wasn't hurting, then we never would've got a chance to talk. I think you're cool, and hopefully you think I'm cool. We go to the same school, so who knows? Maybe this could be the start of a friendship."

Then Ms. Easley, the pageant director, came in.

"Girls, we don't have time for chitter-chatter. You all need to get dressed in opening outfits. We're going to do a run-through."

This was the first time that I got to see Charlotte do her thing on the stage. That girl was posing really cute on the runway. I started out cheering for her until she started her talent. When she sung, she had choreography, and it was like a Broadway stage play. It wasn't some hip-hop number like mine. Hers was more meaningful. I just knew I was going to lose.

***

Three hours later the two of us were standing backstage, getting ready to go out as the two finalists of Miss Teen Charlotte. It was coming down to the questions, and Charlotte was so nervous that she was shaking, and her face was turning pale. The competitor in me vanished. I grabbed her and made her cold body warm as I rubbed her bare shoulders.

"You can do this," I shared. "Whatever they ask you, take in the question. Think of why you want this so bad and nail it."

We were both standing on stage. She did nail the question, and after hearing her answer the question really well, when I was asked the same one, I stuttered. She was crowned Miss Teen Charlotte, and I rushed off stage, feeling like I'd just been played.

***

"Slade! You can't run off the stage, sweetie. You've got to go congratulate the other girls," my mother said, finding me backstage and telling me what I needed to hear, but not what I wanted her to say.

"But Mom—Dad running for mayor—his daughter winner of Miss Teen Charlotte; what a story that was supposed to be. I let him down. I let him down," I repeated, upset.

My mom stroked my cheek and said, "Slade, are you serious, sweetheart? We're proud of you that you got up there. Don't put more on yourself than what needs to be there."

Pulling away from her touch, I huffed, "You don't understand. You've always got everything you've tried for."

"Sweetheart, what are you talking about?" she uttered with compassion.

"When we were at Grandma's house this summer, she showed us the pictures. You were Miss Duke University, and then you went on to be Miss North Carolina in the Miss America pageant."

Placing her arm around me, she would not quit trying to encourage me. "Yes, but I didn't win Miss America. You're not even out of high school. You want to go to college and get in another pageant? That's fine, and it's absolutely nothing wrong with coming in first runner-up."

"I'm not going back out there, Mom."

Then the pagent director started yelling. "Where's the first runner-up? I've never had that happen. Every girl knows there's a possibility that she won't win. *She* doesn't win, and she runs off my stage."

"Here she is, Ms. Easley, ready to go back out there," my mom said as she spun me around, pulled my gown so that it was perfect again, quickly wiped my face, and hugged me tight. He whispered, "Get your tail out there."

Reluctantly I walked back on stage. Though the pageant was over, all the girls were surrounding Charlotte. I hadn't given her a hug. I hadn't congratulated her, and I never thought I had a bad attitude. I wasn't a good sport, but I guess until you don't get something that you really want, you'll never know how you'll act. I wasn't the only one pouting. Girls couldn't even tell me congratulations for being first runner-up. I could hear them saying, "It should've been me as first runner-up. She only got that far because of her father," but I wanted to go all of the way. Now, I had to smile at the queen coming up to me.

"You helped me, and now I've got the crown," Charlotte hugged me and said. "I'm sure it's bittersweet. So thank you."

"Congratulations." I yanked the word out of my mouth. I said all the right things to Charlotte, but then I dashed to the corner off stage under some stairs and just balled my eyes out. I tried to keep my emotions in check, but my dream wasn't going to be realized, and that hurt—like I'd been stabbed over and over and over again. It just felt like I was losing blood and didn't know how to save myself. And then, I heard this husky, male, tenor voice singing the old tune "You Are So Beautiful" to me.

I wiped my tears and looked up. The gorgeous voice equally matched the handsome face with milky way chocolate skin and curly hair.

"Don't worry that you didn't win. You're still beautiful to me."

"Who are you?" I asked.

"Just this guy who's watched a lot of the practices and seen that you're breathtaking."

"What are you talking about?" I said as I started wiping my face and my chest started rising. His every word made me feel good again. "You're just saying that to take pity on me."

"You got a little nervous in the last question. Who would have expected them to ask you the same thing? You heard what she said, and she nailed it, so that would've made anyone nervous. What could you have said differently to make you stand out? But you're a great singer. Who wants to sing Broadway style? You've got soul. You should do something with that. You got on that stage and nailed it. You got everyone on their feet. You're a star."

"And what would you like to be? My agent?"

He leaned down with his lips no more than three inches away from mine and said, "I might want to be more than that."

I felt extremely uncomfortable, so I stood and didn't even realize that my breasts were practically hanging out of the dress. I was giving him all kinds of free views, and I wasn't even trying to do that. When he coughed and motioned for me to look down, I pulled up the dress, but when I looked down at his pants, I could tell there was a connection.

"Thanks for cheering me up," I said. "I did do the best I could."

"And you've got lots of good stuff in you, so shake this off. It's only the beginning. Can I get your number?" he asked.

Before I could say yes or no, we heard this loud bang and then another clang followed by a boom. He dashed away, and I followed him. I came to a halt when he entered a door. In the office of the theater was an older lady being forced into a chair by two big, black guys who looked like they were bodybuilders or bar bouncers or something, and another tough guy was standing in front of her. I was careful not to let them see me, but I could not bring myself to walk away.

"I want my money. Payday is today. Where is my money?" the leader raged.

"I don't know anything about that," the lady uttered.

Then the leader guy slapped her.

"Boots, get your hands off my mom!" the stranger who was just comforting me yelled out. "My boy K.J. told me you'd be flexible."

The Boots dude looked him up and down. "Yeah, flexible on which limb to break if I ain't got my loot. And K.J. trying to make me a record. He crazy anyway. You came to me 'cause you know I'm the only one around here who can give you dough quick. You know what I do if I don't get it."

When I saw how serious this all was, I didn't go in the office, but I didn't want to move away because I didn't want them to hear me. Boots came over and punched him in the gut. The stranger keeled over.

Boots leaned down to him and said, "Today's payday, A.V."

Was A.V. his name? I wondered what it stood for. Then I shook my head, realizing I needed to not care what it stood for. A.V. seemed to be in a mess.

"What are they talking about, son? Payday for what? You told me you got the money from your dad," A.V.'s mom said.

A.V. huffed, "When has he ever given me a thing? I just said that so you wouldn't worry." A.V. turned to Boots. "Y'all didn't have to come up here and demand it. I just need more time."

Boots told him, "Please. I'm not granting it. Just as quick as I gave you the money to keep this theater open, y'all better pay me. And don't say you ain't got it. Y'all on the news with the teen pageants, plays, and concerts going on . . . one event here after the other. Well, I want my money now, because it's due."

"You'll get your money. Just let go of my son," A.V.'s mom begged.

"You won't have a son if I don't get my three Gs." Boots punched A.V. again.

I wanted to help, but at the same time, I didn't need to get involved. Minutes earlier I didn't even know this guy, but now I was sucked into his world, his drama, his pain, and I couldn't pull myself away. I only wished he'd left me on the stairs, bawlin' my eyes out alone and secluded.

CHAPTER TWO
SCREAM

One hard punch after another struck the stranger who'd serenaded me. It was tough to watch him get beat up so hard. I was so shocked that I didn't even realize I screamed.

"Who was that?" Boots angrily belted out.

"Don't hit him anymore!" I yelled, now understanding that I could not back away.

"Run!" A.V. shouted out to me.

I didn't move. "You can't hurt him anymore."

"Get her!" Boots yelled out to his two thug partners.

"No, no, no, don't hurt her. I'll talk to her. I'll keep her quiet," A.V. shouted before the thugs got to me.

He struggled to come to the door because he was beaten up. The other guys were looming, waiting on the stranger to let me go so that they could get me in check. Their glares made me uneasy, but I kept my cool.

"The police are on the way in," I lied out of instinct to try to scare them off.

I must have displayed a great poker face, because they believed me. Boots snapped and eyed A.V., giving the sign that this wasn't over. Then the three of them rushed past me.

"You shouldn't be here," A.V. said to me as I exhaled.

"Oh my gosh, are you okay?" I said, ignoring his concern about me. I was ten times more worried about him.

"Fine," he huffed with a bit of an attitude.

Blood was gushing from his mouth, and he was holding his ribs like something was broken. Concerned, I voiced, "We've got to get you to a hospital."

"No, no really . . . you've got to go."

"I'm going to go tell my dad. He knows important people in the city. It's going to be fine. He'll get the police to catch these guys. They can't just come in here and beat people up like this, ransacking your mother's office. This is horrible," I said.

"No, you've got to stay out of it."

"You don't understand. This just happened to my house not too long ago. People just think because they're big and tough or going through stuff that they can make other peoples' lives miserable. My father won't stand for this."

I was serious too. My sisters didn't like folks knowing our dad was powerful, but I had no problem letting the world know. My dad had us helping him get elected. He was happy to show the city he had a nice family. Now it was my time to get him to help.

"Look, you don't understand," he said more forcefully.

His mother sashayed her way over to the door, hand on hip, eyes bloodshot red. I stuck out my hand to introduce myself, believing that she couldn't be angry with me. After all, I was trying to help.

His mother started yelling. "How dare you come in here and stick your nose all in where it doesn't belong. Isn't the pageant over? What are you doing way back here anyway? This part is off limits. We don't want the police involved."

"But they were beating up your son," I said to her as if she hadn't just been in the same room as me.

The way she was positioned in the room, she was behind her boy. She saw him getting punched, but she couldn't see the damage. He wasn't trying to show her, either.

She screamed, "Listen girl, it's none of your business."

"Mom, you don't have to be so rough," A.V. said to his mom, finally looking her way.

"Well, who is this girl? And what have you gotten yourself into with these guys?" She turned him around and saw up close he was really banged up. "Oh my gosh, son. I don't know this chick, but she's right . . . you need to get to a hospital."

"It's fine, Mom," he said as he keeled over in pain.

She lifted up his shirt, and his fine caramel brown skin had a dark red and blue mark on his left ribs. I squinted, seeing the wound. When his mom touched him, she assessed it wasn't broken, just deeply bruised.

"Sit down, son. I'm gonna get an ice pack out of my freezer to put it on you," she said. "I need to hurry up so I can get out there and meet the lady over the pageant to get the rest of her payment."

"So you guys are just going to do nothing?" I said to him, when his mom was farther away. "What if those guys come back?"

In frustration, he said, "They're coming back. But you need to get out of here. You don't need to say nothing."

"Hello? Hello?" I heard Ms. Easley call out from down the hall. "I'm looking for one of our contestants. I've got parents trying to find their daughter. Slade Sharp, are you back here?"

"Sharp?" his mother asked as she threw her son the blue ready-made ice pack and came charging at me. "You one of those mayoral candidate's daughters? Shoot, this is not what we need. You little privileged, stuck up wench. Don't you speak a word of what you've seen here tonight. I'm going to go divert her, have her look for you someplace else, and you get on out there where you should be with your parents. I don't need no trouble for my theater. Am I making myself clear?"

All I could do was nod my head as she headed into the hallway. She was treating me like I was the enemy, like I beat up her son and squeezed her throat. I was trying to get them help. All the name calling wasn't necessary.

"Ouch," A.V. said when he put ice on his wound.

I was supposed to be leaving. Instead, I went over to him.

"I was just trying to help. Like now, you're struggling. Let me help," I uttered, still feeling a connection.

"You've got to get out of here. I don't know how much you saw, but those guys are nobody to play with. I made some bad decisions trying to help my mom out, but we don't want your family involved."

"I just think it wasn't right, and I plan to help, okay?" I said as I lifted my hands up in the air and turned to walk away toward the door. He grabbed my arm and clutched it real tight, almost hurting me. "Let me go!"

"I can't have you getting . . ."

Suddenly, I heard my father's voice at the door say, "Hey you, you need to let my daughter's arm go! Slade, what's going on here? Your mother and I have been looking for you everywhere."

A.V. released my arm, and I said, "Nothing's going on, Daddy."

My father sighed, "You standing here talking to some guy who's bruised up, and he's grabbing on you all crazy . . . go on out there to your mom."

"Dad . . ."

My dad walked in and got closer to the stranger. "What's your name, young man?"

"I don't have to tell you nothing, sir."

"Oh, that's how you gonna play this?" My

dad pulled out his phone. "You don't have to tell me your name, but you can tell the police . . . assaulting my daughter."

"Dad! Please!" I shouted out.

"And you thought he was going to help me?" A.V. barked my way.

My father took a few steps back. "Help you? You're assaulting my child, and you think I'm going to help you?"

"Daddy, he didn't assault me. He just wants me to stay out of his business."

"Well that sounds like something he said that I can agree on. Let's go," my father told me. When we got to the door to exit the office, he turned back around. "And you, young man, stay away from my baby. You think you have problems now, but you ain't seen problems."

"Dad!" I uttered, shocked.

The guy just shook his head. I wanted to apologize. I wanted to tend to him. I wanted to tell my dad what I had really witnessed so he could direct his anger in the right place. But it had been a crazy night. Now, not only had I lost the pageant that I cared a lot about, walking out of the theater, I realized that I lost a friend that I never had. Something in his eyes—the sadness there when I was leaving—I couldn't shake. But I was going to have to forget him because he wanted nothing to do with me. And my father wanted me to have nothing to do with him.

***

Most would think my life wasn't bad . . . sitting in a limousine, riding along with my privileged family. However, it felt like I was in a big coffin, not some plush, luxurious car. I felt smothered. My parents' eyes were staring down at me. My sisters were looking at me all cross-eyed and crazy. If their looks could kill, I'd be dead.

Frustrated, I just yelled, "Say whatever you have to say already! I'm sick of being scrutinized by y'all. Nobody in this car is perfect!"

"None of y'all want to tell her? I'll tell her. Sharp girls have standards, Slade. You lost the pageant. You dashed off the stage. You're supposed to lose with dignity and grace. Yeah you came back on, but Mom had to go get you," my younger sister Sloan stated.

"Oh, so I just embarrassed everybody. Is that it?" I asked, half caring.

"She's not trying to hurt your feelings, but . . ." Yuri added, before she stopped.

I said, "But what, Yuri? Spit it out."

"She doesn't need to spit it out," Shelby said as she hunched her shoulder like she was sick of me. "Everything isn't going to always go your way, Slade, but you know you can't pout about it . . . and you sort of did, sis. Love you to pieces, but you sort of did."

Ansli was sitting near me, and she slid a little closer in and put her arm around me. "I know how it feels to have the world you envision in your mind fall apart. And if you thought you were going to win and didn't, it's got to be hard, but you did really good. We all were just a little shocked when you acted the way you did."

"She needs to get over it. She went MIA for a long time," Sloan uttered. "Selfish butt."

"Screw you, Sloan," I let slip from my mouth.

"Alright girls that's quite enough," my mom said with a stern voice, clearly disappointed in us both.

"No, no, that's not enough, Sherri," my dad said. "We need to talk to you young ladies about these boys."

My eyes bucked wide. Only my father knew about the stranger. He said that I could never see him again, so he didn't need to bring it up.

"I can't say for sure that I'm going to win anything because these polls tell you one thing, but the election results may turn out to be another. But if this election goes the way it's predicted, you all are going to have to be smart. There're going to be all kinds of young men trying to get with you girls. You can't just fall for some cute guy with muscles, follow him anywhere, and end up getting killed. I raised all five of you to be independent, to have your own dreams and your own goals, not to be around here excited about chasing boys."

"Dad, I don't know what you're talking about, but I'm not into the boys. I'm focused on trying to be summa cum laude of my graduating class in two and a half years," Sloan said, as if he was offending her.

Knowing this was all directed at me, I

huffed, "Well, Dad, you misjudged Shelby's boyfriend, thinking he was a thug because he was fighting at the political debate. Turns out he was only defending his mom against an abusive stepfather. And then there's Ansli's boyfriend, and for some reason you're really cool with him. You don't even judge him for being homeless."

"What are you trying to say?" Ansli said to me.

Feeling bad that I upset the wrong sister, I uttered, "I'm not trying to offend you or anything. I'm just saying that boys have tough situations, but that doesn't mean they're bad boys we need to stay away from. And just because I was talking to somebody doesn't mean I was trying to sleep with them."

"Slade!" my mom said in an appalled tone.

The limousine couldn't have gotten to our home any faster. I couldn't wait to get out of the stuffy car. As soon as it parked in our circular driveway, I jumped out.

"You better talk to that girl!" I heard my dad say to my mom as I started walking down our long driveway toward the street.

My mom called out, "Slade, come back here so you can get your stuff out of the car. Nobody's going to carry your stuff into the house, girl."

"Isn't that what a limousine driver is for?" I yelled.

"Slade, get your tail back up here. Your mom wasn't asking you," my dad shouted.

So I turned back around. I was so frustrated. My head was pounding.

"We got it," Shelby said, as my sisters got all of my pageant wear.

"Good girls. Take that stuff on in so I can talk some sense into your sister."

"Talk some sense into me?" I questioned, feeling like I was growing in the moonlight and wasn't trying to let anyone, even my mom, belittle me.

"Yes, honey. I was glad you came back out and congratulated the queen, but I don't know what's going on with you. Sometimes you make me want to scream. I know teenage girls are a handful, but you I don't understand. At least Sloan tells me what she's thinking, and Shelby makes a case for what she wants. You, you just try to be some maverick. And don't get it twisted. That may be your school mascot, but it's not reality. You don't run anything around here. You just can't go off when you want to. We searched after the pageant over thirty minutes looking for you. We didn't know if someone had snatched you up or what."

"Snatched me up, Mom? Really?"

"Yes, really. There were some strange characters, and nobody knew who they were, and we couldn't find you. You're a gorgeous girl, and you were very depressed. I was worried. Just don't hold your emotions so close to your chest, Slade. It's time to grow up a little bit, babe," she said.

She patted me on the shoulder and left me outside to think. I looked up at the beautiful, early October evening sky, and my heart longed for the night to give me direction. Of all the sisters, I had been the one who stood on my faith the most. I wasn't overly religious or anything, but the gospel hymns my grandmother used to sing stuck with me, and I believed the words. But it had been a long time since I sung any of them. Now more than anything I needed the Lord to show up, so I started singing an old treasure that always gave me hope, "Pass Me Not, O Gentle Savior." I sang:

"Pass me not, O gentle Savior, Hear my humble cry; While on others Thou art calling, Do not pass me by. Savior, Savior, Hear my humble cry; While on others Thou art calling, Do not pass me by. "

Then I stopped singing and shouted. "I don't have any friends. I don't have a crown. I don't have my dreams. Could You help give me a life?"

About thirty minutes later, after I had taken a bath, I turned on my computer to see what I had been missing. I had an e-mail from the queen. "Call me. Let's be friends," Charlotte wrote.

I wanted to yell, "You're the last person I want to be friends with!" So I turned off the computer and went to bed, hoping that the stranger was okay. He wouldn't leave my mind.

***

I wasn't a fan of school, but I sure loved being in glee class. It was a combination of singing, acting, and dancing all in one. My skinny, strawberry-blonde teacher Ms. Oxford had been on Broadway herself. She talked in an Irish accent, but used slang like she was from Harlem. The class was mixed, with a diverse group of characters. Jocks, geeks, all races, sizes, and genders too. If you had spunk and talent, the class was for you.

We'd only been in school a little over a month and a half, but I still didn't have any real buddies. When three girls, whom I called a modern day TLC because they were cute, cool, and charming, walked in, I caught myself staring. I didn't know much more about them besides that they were juniors like me, but their friendship was one I longed to be a part of. They were huddled up, laughing. I was so into looking at the sassy threesome that I didn't even realize that we had a guest enter the room. Everybody rushing up to shake his hand, like he was somebody important.

Ms. Oxford said, "So, I can tell all that hand-shaking means you're giving somebody mad respect. You must know who he is."

"Yeah, Mr. Mundy from Mundy Records," a dude from the back shouted out.

"That's exactly correct. The record label that's known for breaking new talent in the city of Charlotte. And he's here today to talk to you guys about something special. So without further ado, I turn the mic over to Mr. Brian Mundy," Ms. Oxford said.

Everyone around me stood, clapping. The opportunity to be signed to a record label was a dream come true. Mr. Mundy motioned for us to sit.

The tall, handsome, well-dressed man in his forties said, "Why, thank you guys. You all appreciate that I have a business that puts out records. Well, I couldn't do what I do without great talent, so I am in awe of you. Your teacher has been sending me demos. Anyway, let me say she has inspired me to go ahead and start another big talent search, and I am only inviting select schools that have people in glee club to enter. I need to put out a new hit. It's hard times even in the record business, so I'm just going to be real with you guys. If you got your 'A' game, and you're ready to break out and do big things, then you might win this contest."

"What is the winner of the contest going to get?" the same guy from the back shouted out.

"What's your name, young man?"

"You want to know my real name or my stage name?" my classmate asked.

"I want to know whatever name you want me to know," Mr. Mundy said.

"Oh, then I'm Flo Breaker."

"Oh, you from Florida?" Mr. Mundy sought to confirm.

"That's right."

"Wow, that's wassup. You can't steal the Florida name and not bring it."

"I can sing, but I want to be a rapper."

"Alright, alright, I'm going to be real honest. I am looking to sign a male soloist or a female group."

The threesome in the front was all giddy. They were waving their hands and bumping each other. They looked real desperate trying to get his attention.

Finally, he looked at them and said, "Unless there is another member of your group or one of y'all isn't in it, I've got to be honest again, I'm not that interested."

The shortest one in the middle, whose name I think was Taylor, asked, "Why not?"

He answered, "Because I like even numbered female groups. It just keeps the drama under control."

The one with spunk said, "Sir, I'm Dayna, and you need to hear us first. We bring it, we are good, and we're just what you need for your label."

"Alright, but I'm already telling you."

Ms. Oxford cut in and said, "Yeah girls, you've got to understand when a record label is telling you what they want, don't try to give them what you have. Figure it out. There's plenty of talent in this room. You need to add somebody to the group if y'all need to pair up."

"But I don't even need to try." Flo Breaker uttered in a melancholy tone.

"You told me you're a rapper and a singer.

I might be interested. All of you, if your group is phenomenal, if you're something other than what I am looking for, then you got to go for it. You've got to believe in yourself. You've got to make me as an executive want to change my mind. But just know my eye is going to be looking out for a female group that is even in number or a male singer. I don't care if he's singing country or R&B, but I do want him to sing. If you guys have any more questions, I will be here for a little while, but start singing, start practicing. Here's the catch, competition is next week. Your teacher has all the particulars."

Finally when Mr. Mundy was gone our teacher told us to line up. We needed to practice our chords and sing some. I just happened to be standing near the threesome. I don't know if I was a little too loud or what, but they looked at me like I had the plague.

Caylen, the third member of the group, said, "We need to talk to you as soon as class is over."

"Okay," I said.

"Okay, focus young people. Let's go," Ms. Oxford said, knowing that rehearsal was gonna be hard, as we all were in dreamland.

But it seemed like it was taking forever. I had no idea what they wanted to talk to me about.

When the bell rang, Dayna and the others stepped right over to me and said, "Look, you tryna get a record deal?"

"Yeah," I said. "But I'm not even trying for the contest because I'm not in a group."

"Well, you hear what he told us?" Taylor said in a sweeter tone.

"Yes, that you've got an odd number," I replied.

"Right, we need one more to be a modern day En Vogue. Do you want to be in our group?" Dayna asked.

Looking at the three of them and thinking I could be a part of their group made me all excited. I'd heard them sing during class. They had skills, and I guess today they finally heard. And though I always wanted to be a solo act, if being in a group could get me out there, then maybe that's what I needed to do. Like my grandma always said, "Nothing was wrong with casting my net on the other side of the boat to catch fish." After all, Beyoncé started in a group.

So I looked at the three of them and said, "Yeah, I'll be the fourth member of your group. Let's go win this thing."

Taylor hugged me. Dayna and Caylen gave each other high fives. Then the four of us let out a loud scream.

CHAPTER THREE
SWAGGER

"You want to go where, Slade?" my mom asked a couple days after our blowup.

"I've been invited to a slumber party."

"You're sixteen, honey. You know I don't allow you girls to stay at other people's houses," she said, not moved by my disappointed face. "Besides, the answer is also no because I don't even know who you're even talking about."

"It's a girl named Taylor who is in my class. Her mom is an elementary school teacher. She wants you to call her so you feel comfortable about the situation. I said we'd call back. Please,

Mom, please!"

"No, Slade, you know it's a rule that I have. I can control what goes on here, and you can invite your new friends here, but I'm not allowing you to go to somebody else's house. You're just not going."

I wasn't trying to get all big and bad with my mom, but she was wrong. I was sixteen, and since I was almost seventeen, it was about time I stood up for what I believed in. She was an attorney. I had to speak her language and make a case for why she needed to chill.

"What are you afraid of, Mom? You raised me right. I'm not going to be influenced by anybody else. Plus, her mom is a teacher at an elementary school. She teaches music, for goodness sake. It's a two-parent family."

"That doesn't matter to me."

"I'm just giving you all the facts. It's a good home. She doesn't have an older brother. No one is going to be walking around naked."

"Watch your mouth, girl."

Irritated, I said, "I'm just sayin'. You have nothing to fear. I gotta grow up sometime,

Mom, and make my own friends. The Sharp sisters are tight. With Dad running for mayor and all, the whole city knows that, but you know I'm the outsider. That's why I hang with you more than anybody else. Shelby and Ansli pair up, Sloan and Yuri pair up, and then it's just me. I finally found some girls my age that want to hang with me, some other juniors that want me to be in a singing group with them."

"You want to be in a group now? Slade, really?"

"Mom, come on. Let me try my passion. I'm just asking for one night. Progress reports came out. I've got all As and one B. My room is spotless. I never give you any trouble. Give me a little leeway. Haven't I earned that?"

"Alright, alright, I'll see, but I can't believe you have me dealing with this now. You girls know I'm stressed dealing with this election. Get her mom on the phone."

Thankfully, the two career women talked like they'd known each other for a long time. They were definitely cut from the same cloth, and my mom felt comfortable that I could go, even though she did insist on dropping me off and meeting the rest of the girls.

***

The girls' reactions upon seeing me varied. Taylor was all excited to see me, and she reached out and gave me a hug. I guess I just assumed that the other two girls were on board with it; after all we had to practice, we had to bond, we had to really be a group. But I sensed—since their noses were all up in the air and their eyes were staring me down like I was the enemy or something—that Dayna and Caylen weren't too happy to have me there.

When Taylor told me to follow her to her room to put down my bag, I just shot a straight look at her and got right to the point. "Do Dayna and Caylen not want me here or something?"

Almost laughing, like what I said was crazy, Taylor uttered, "No, that's just how they are. The three of us have been tight for so long. Forgive them."

"No, and I'm uncomfortable. I'm not trying

to push myself on nobody," I told her as I rolled my eyes.

Trying to calm me by nudging me a bit, Taylor said, "You heard Mr. Mundy. He's only looking for an even-numbered female group. They need you."

Standing boldly to not budge in my thinking, I responded, "Oh, so I'm supposed to be okay with however they treat me?"

"You want to sing, and without you the three of us are good. With you . . . we can be great. So much is on the line. We just need to put aside all the drama. Let's get to know each other . . . it'll be fun!" Taylor put her arm underneath mine and escorted me into the basement.

"So does this mean we can do what we've always done?" Dayna said to Taylor.

"Of course we can. If Slade is going to be one of us she's got to go through with the ritual," Taylor replied.

"Then what are you waiting for? Why didn't you put the video in?" Caylen asked.

"What video?" I yelled from across the room. I didn't know if they were trying to keep it a secret or what, but I heard them, so I asked.

Caylen asked, "Where is it, Taylor? Let me just pop it in. You think she can fit in with us?"

In a rude voice, Dayna said, "We'll see."

Taylor went behind the couch and pulled out a folder. She handed Dayna a DVD, and the three of them got all cozy in front of the TV. When the screen came on, there was a girl undressing in front of another girl who was already nude with a guy lying there looking. The two girls started making out, and the three of them were laughing. They didn't seem to be aroused. They were, for sure, amused, but I was completely uncomfortable and didn't understand what all this was about.

"Look over at Miss Prissy turning red," Dayna teased.

"Are you a virgin, Slade?" Caylen asked me in a real seductive and weird kind of way. I just frowned at her like it was none of their business.

"I told you she wasn't our kind of girl," Dayna said to Taylor.

With much attitude, I gasped, "Well I don't know what your kind of girl is, but if y'all trying to feel all up on me and do some freaky girly night out, I'm not in."

Then Dayna got up in my face and said, "What? You calling us freaks?"

Stepping up even closer to her, I said, "If the shoe fits."

She pushed me. I pushed her back. I didn't know who Dayna thought I was, but a punk wasn't it.

Taylor stood firm between us and said, "Okay, okay, stop you guys! Listen. Slade, we do this because we're trying to get great moves. Yes, we went to a producer's house one time, and he told us watching this kind of stuff relaxes us, makes our bodies all loose so we can be better artists. So, that's what we're doing. Nothing more, nothing less. No one is trying to touch you or have you touch them."

"And you believe this guy?" I uttered, thinking that was ludicrous.

"Regardless, watching this is fun, and I don't got no problem saying I like it," Dayna tried to get in my face and say.

"Well, if you got a good voice, who cares

how you work it? Turn on a dang mic and let's practice. You want me out of this group? If we don't have any harmony, I'm out anyway. I don't have to just conform to y'all's ways. You got to conform to mine too. I've got talent. Y'all asked me to be in the group," I said.

I went over to the TV, turned it off, turned the radio on, and started singing whatever was on. It was an old tune by Destiny's Child, "Survivor," but when they got up and started singing with me, something clicked. I thought I wanted to walk out, but the sound the four of us made was a groove I couldn't get without them, and I didn't want to.

***

"You can't break up with me. I love you. I've given you money. I made you feel good. Now, you're just going to dump me? What's this about? Another girl or something? It's nobody that's going to treat you like I am," I heard Taylor cry out.

She was so upset. She actually awoke me from my sleep. The four of us had conked out on her family room floor. I looked over and saw Dayna snoring and Caylen slobbering. I didn't want to get in Taylor's business, but she had it going on. The last thing she needed to be doing was getting all upset over some guy. So, I went up to her and motioned for her to hang up.

"Huh?" she said with her ear still to the receiver.

I held my fingers like a phone and placed my hand down like I was hanging up. I was real adamant. Later for that loser. His loss.

"Alright, fine. I've got to go," she finally said, and as she hung up the phone, she fell right into my arms. "He just broke up with me like that. I don't understand."

"I don't know much about your boyfriend— how long y'all been dating or anything like that—but you are too strong to be stressed over somebody who doesn't want to be with you. Forget him. We're trying to get a record deal anyway, right?" I tried to encourage her and say.

"Yeah," she said as she leaned up.

I wiped her tears away and voiced, "How can we get a record deal if you are still focused on getting a man? If you could only have one or the other, which would it be?"

"I wanted both," Taylor boldly stated.

"Well, you can't get it all in this life. My parents tell me that all the time."

Pushing me off, she said, "Whatever, your dad's about to be the mayor."

"Maybe, maybe not. But I know more than anything that I want to sing. I want to be an artist. I want to sell millions of albums. I want to make it big. I thought it was going to be as a solo artist, but now I'm open to this group, and I like the sound we're making as a unit. I don't want to be in a group with somebody who's focused on some guy who's weighing her down, and every five minutes something is going to have her stressed. Let him go, and and when you do, he'll come beggin'."

"You think?" she said with hope.

"Wait, that's not why you do it, Taylor. You don't let him go so he'll want you. You let him go because he's not good for you."

"I gave him so much, and I'm not going to be anything without him."

"Oh, Taylor, really? Come on, girl." I took her hand and dragged her over to the mirror. "Look at yourself. That's right . . . go on, look."

"What am I looking at? I'm a basket case," she said as she wiped tears.

"But you're still a beautiful basket case. You got to believe your worth. You've got to stay focused on your dream. You've got to get your attitude and your swagger back. A guy can break up with you, but he shouldn't be able to break you."

"You think this is easy?" she asked as I stayed quiet. "What, you got a boyfriend?"

Cracking a smile, I uttered, "It's this guy I saw a few days back. I'll probably never see him again, but he got to me. I was in this contest, and I didn't win. That's why I can tell you, you don't get everything. I didn't know that right after I would meet the owner of a record label who would give me an opportunity to be in a group with you guys. I thought there was only one way I could accomplish my dream, but when that door closed, another one opened. If I had stayed down and not taken the help of a stranger to lift me up, then I wouldn't have been ready to jump into something new with you guys. And as crazy as your crew is, I like this. Well, some of it, anyway. All of that video, movie stuff . . . that ain't me."

"Thank you," Taylor said as she stroked my arm. "I'm going to be okay, huh?"

"Yes, you're going to be okay. With or without him, Taylor is going to be okay," I encouraged as she hugged me.

"What y'all talkin' about all loud, waking people up and stuff?" grumpy Dayna asked.

It's like the girl always had an attitude. Pulling away from the hug, Taylor rolled her eyes hard my way. I hated that she was so tense.

"Dayna, give me my caterpillar!" Caylen screamed out.

"Girl, wake up. You're talking in your sleep," Dayna said as she took a pillow and bopped Caylen on top of the head.

"Let's have some munchies. Girl time!" Taylor said. Then she peered my way. "I'm feeling better thanks to somebody. Oh, I'm so glad you're in this group!"

Taylor gave me a thumbs-up before she went out to get snacks. Dayna was still staring at me, and it was not in a cool, fun, receptive way. Her eyes seemed full of hate.

Tired of the tension, I approached Dayna and said, "What's up? Why do you still have a beef with me? I thought we squashed all of that. We just sung our hearts out. We're trying to be a group here, and I sense that whatever I do you don't want that."

"I don't need you trying to be the hero with Taylor."

"Did you hear the whole conversation? You want me to let her stay down, and stay upset, and stay a basket case?"

"Just forget it."

"No, no. Say what you have to say to me."

"You don't even know much about a boy-friend. You ain't even had one. You cringed at the sight of someone having sex."

"I don't want to watch it. I want to do it."

"So then you haven't ever done it."

"Oh, forget it."

Dayna wouldn't let me walk away. "You were

talking about a guy. You want to get close. You want to be cool. You want this group thing to work . . . then don't be such a closed onion. Peel back some layers."

"Oh, look at you trying to be all literary," Caylen teased.

Dayna winked at her and said, "Just trying to use some analogies so I can get some good marks on my SATs."

"What do you want to know?" I asked her.

"The guy you were talking about. Is he your boyfriend? You said you were in a contest? What kind of contest? Who's the mystery guy?" Dayna asked.

"It doesn't matter. I'll probably never see him again."

"Yeah, I got that part, but who is he?"

"I mean, I don't even know his name. I was running for Miss Teen Charlotte at this theater. I lost, and I was all upset. Backstage he just came up to me, and he was everything."

"You met him where? Backstage at the Ren . . ." Caylen started saying, but Dayna covered her mouth.

"I think you might see him again. You believe in destiny, don't you?" Dayna cryptically
told me.

Dayna lifted her hand in the air and wanted
me to give her a high-five. All of a sudden, she
went from cold to warm with me. I so wanted to
believe what Dayna was saying about my mystery man. Though I believed for myself what I
told Taylor about not needing a guy, if I were
able to see the one that turned my frown into a
smile again, it'd be on.

***

"So you really want to be in a singing group?"
my sister Sloan asked me the morning of our big
audition, giving me no privacy in the bathroom
to get ready.

"Y'all have been in here forever," Yuri said,
joining us. "I've got to get ready for school too."

"We're having a deep conversation in here,
Yuri," Sloan told her as she washed her face.

"What about the whole singing thing?
We've seen those girls at school. They just don't
look like your kind of people," Yuri said. "Plus,

Slade, we don't have you around as much."

"Yuri, what's my kind of people?" I asked, cracking up at them having a hard time saying what their body language was displaying.

They would never admit it, but they missed me. Though they were like two pieces of bread stuck together, I was the flavor, the medium. I was the peanut butter and jelly. Dagonit, the bologna and mayonnaise. I made their world fun. Though I felt they didn't need me, it was pretty nice to know they wanted me around.

Seeing they weren't into talking about people, I said, "To answer your question, yes, I want to be in a singing group, but I don't know how it's going to work with these girls. I've got my doubts, too, but if you could just hear us."

"Well, you've been practicing with them for the last week nonstop."

"We've been talking about coming to your audition today, Shelby and Ansli too."

"Really?" I said, truly shocked.

I'd love their support, but I didn't dare ask for it. They were all so busy—particularly my two older sisters—to even think about taking time to support me. It had been like pulling teeth to get them to come to the pageant.

"I don't know where this place is. The record owner had to change the place a couple times, but when I get all the information, I'll text it to you guys. I'm glad you're coming!" I said as I hugged the two of them.

"We want you to be happy," Yuri said.

I uttered, "I'm going to get on stage today and give it my all."

"You could be a day away from getting a record deal," Sloan said.

"If you get one, does that mean you'll move out?" Yuri asked.

"I don't know. If we blow up, maybe."

***

After school and before the tryout, we went to Taylor's mom's school to get ready. Just as we were approaching, we heard yelling coming from her mom's music classroom.

"But you can't get rid of the arts program! If you do that, what are these kids going to have? Some of them, that's all they're good at. It helps them do better in other subjects. Who do I need to talk to about this? The decision can't be final," Taylor's mom argued.

"Mrs. Dale, you need to calm down. It's not a done deal yet, but it looks like that's the way it's leaning. I just didn't want you to be caught off guard. I thought you deserved to know. You've been the backbone of this school for years now. You and I both know the kids who go here are economically challenged, and I agree with you that the arts lift their spirits, but if the board cuts the funding, it's out of my control. I'm going to have to let you go," the principal told her.

"When is the vote?" her mom said.

"In a couple of weeks."

"Are you kidding me? So in the middle of the school year, they're just going to drop music?"

Taylor rushed into the classroom. The three of us followed. She hugged her mom, and the two of them began to cry. I probably couldn't understand everything that this class meant to them, but I could tell the school was old, and I could remember that she told me her mom had been here since the beginning. I detested that some people felt that the arts were expendable. If it helps to free a person's mind and gets a child to extend his or her creativity and positivity in life, why in the world would a school district cut it? Shouldn't they look at cutting people's salaries instead of a program that touches lives?

The principal left, saying, "I'm sorry. I need to get to a meeting."

My heart broke as I watched Taylor console her mom. I so wanted to help. I smiled, seeing their connection was strong.

"Listen," her mom finally said as they pulled apart. "You girls have to go get to that audition."

"But, Mom," Taylor said in a caring tone, "What are you going to do if they cut the program?"

Mrs. Dale explained, "I'm not going to focus on that right now, and I don't want you to focus on it either. I hate that you overheard it, but you've got to forget about it. Get it out of your mind."

Her mom walked over to the piano and started striking chords. On her snap count, the four of us started warming up. We had a dope sound. Her mom certainly needed to be a music teacher. She was on it.

Mrs. Dale stopped playing and said, "You're ready. Go get them. I'm going to finish up here, and then I'm going to make some calls. I don't think I'm going to be able to make it, but I know you'll give me great news."

Taylor didn't want to leave her mom, but Dayna and Caylen pulled her away. I knew it wasn't just about the money, though being without a job these days certainly wasn't a good thing. It was about the passion her mom had for what she did. Shame on the school board for wanting to take that away.

I'd been asking Dayna for days for the address to where we were going to the audition because I wanted to tell my sisters. When we pulled up to the same theater I was at for the pageant, I was surprised. Immediately, I texted it to my sisters, hoping they would have enough time to be here.

When we stepped inside, the guy I thought I would never see again was standing on the stage, working a crowd with his hips to his lips.

I remembered him serenading me, but I never even imagined that we had the same dream. I didn't even realize I was smiling all over, but how could I help it? His voice melted my heart, and his sound made me dance. He had amazing swagger.

CHAPTER FOUR
SNAKE

"Slade, Taylor . . . snap out of it. We've got to get backstage," Dayna said to the two of us.

It was so hard for me to take my eyes off of that superb performance. We had a good show prepared, but how in the world were we going to top that? Honestly, I wouldn't be upset if the hottie won the contest over us. That's just how strong of a connection I felt to the guy.

As we were walking down the back corridor, Dayna turned around and said, "You know you've got to be initiated into the group."

"I thought that's what watching all of those

crazy DVDs was about. I'm fully in," I said as I cocked my head and looked at her like she was tripping.

"Nope," Dayna said as she puffed up her lips. "Now you got to put some of those skills to work."

"We're about to go on stage. Shouldn't we be concentrating on that?" Taylor said.

"Exactly," I replied, happy somebody had some sense.

Dayna gave Caylen a real cold stare, which made Caylen speak up. "Yeah, um, ya know, Dayna's right. It's only fair. Right before a performance is when you've got to really show us you want to be a part of the group; so either you're in or you're out."

"What do you want me to do?" I asked, really fed up, knowing that I just wouldn't do any ol' thing.

"Yeah, I mean come on, Dayna. I'm ready to win this thing. And as you just saw, it's not going to be easy," Taylor said. "Besides, Sloan needs to really concentrate."

Dayna argued, "I'm just saying. It's only fair,

and she needs to flirt with the next guy who comes around here."

"No . . ." Taylor uttered. "We need to continue doing the steps because y'all changed some. The stage is larger than what we thought we were going to have, so . . ."

"No, no, no, it's fine," I said, cutting her off as I completely changed my view of their hazing when I saw the stranger coming our way. "I have no problem complying. I'll show you I want to be in the group."

"Yeah, show us," Dayna said as her head was looking in the same direction as mine.

I walked straight up to A.V., placed my hand on his chest, rubbed it, felt his abs, and said, "You are so sexy. You got up on that stage, and you made me lose my mind."

I leaned in and nibbled on his ear a little bit. I didn't even know the guy, but I was all into the challenge. He was smiling.

I continued flirting. "I think you are fine, and you sing darn good too."

All of a sudden, pandemonium broke out when Taylor rushed beside me and pushed my hand away. "What are you doing? Why are you touching him like that?"

I said, "What do you mean? You know what I'm doing. I'm showing you I can rise to the occasion."

Taylor confused me when she looked at the stranger and yelled, "How could you stand there and let her do that? You see me here, but you're smiling like you enjoy this."

He looked away. She dashed off. Then Dayna smiled my way.

"I think the friendship you were building with my girl, trying to be closer to her than me, is over," Dayna said nastily to my face before following Taylor.

I wanted clarity. Caylen was the only one in the group still around. As I stepped toward her for answers, she dashed away too.

Frustrated, I uttered, "What in the world is going on? They gave me a challenge. I know it seemed weird coming on to you like that, but that's what they wanted me to do. What was I thinking?"

"So you didn't mean it?" he playfully asked.

"I mean, how can I even like you when you told me to mind my own business? Besides, you didn't even tell me your name. But I heard it in the argument, A.V."

"A.V.? My name is Avery. Avery Hardy."

Sitting down on the same stairs I was on just weeks earlier to make sense of everything, I said, "I guess I heard it wrong. Avery, what in the world was all that about?"

"Um, I didn't know you guys knew each other," he said.

"Yeah, I'm in a group with them."

"It was just the three of them in a group. When did they add another member?"

"So you know them?"

"Taylor is my ex."

My mouth hung open. "Wait a minute. You're the guy who just broke up with her a couple of days ago?"

Understanding everything, I ran to find them. As soon as I did, Caylen had her arm around Taylor, consoling her. As if Dayna was waiting on me to arrive, she gave me a smirk. I went right up to Taylor.

"I didn't know he was your boyfriend."

"That's the same guy I was telling you about."

"I, I, I had no clue he was yours. I mean . . ."

Taylor lashed out. "What do you mean you had no clue? There were pictures of him all in my room."

"We weren't in your room long! We spent the majority of the night downstairs! I had no idea what your boyfriend even looked like. Come on, think about this, if I knew he was your man, I wouldn't try to get with him."

"Yes you would. That's why you were telling me to forget him. I didn't need him, so he'd be free for you to have."

"That's not true."

"Sounds like it to me," Dayna said, wanting to make this a huge problem.

"Who said I was asking you?" I yelled, understanding now that she set me up the whole time.

Taylor looked my way. "Can we just talk about this later? We're going to go on in a few minutes, and I don't want this upsetting me. I saw the way you were looking at him when he was on stage, like you were drooling, wanted to lick him all over or something. It was just nasty. I didn't understand it, but now I get it. You want my boo."

"Well you kept calling him my boo so I didn't even know his name was Avery."

"Well, you're calling him Avery now," Dayna uttered, again adding two cents that no one asked her for.

"Because he just told me his name. Shoot, I thought it was A.V.," I yelled in the face of the girl whom I wanted to punch.

Dayna said, "Ugh, real convenient. Everyone knows Avery Hardy. He's all over YouTube."

"Come on, Taylor," I said, truly not wanting to lose her friendship over this misunderstanding.

Yeah, in my mind I was attracted to this guy, but I never thought I would see him again anyway. So I cut him off, stopped the feelings that I had from flowing, and put him out of my mind. I could do that because I had never had a true girlfriend, only my sisters, but I was enjoying what Taylor and I were building. Certainly, she had to feel that too.

"You've got to forgive me. We've got to get up there and sing," I said, trying to convince the leader.

"We're not getting up anywhere and singing no note together ever again. You're out of the group," Taylor coldly blurted out.

She walked away, taking her two goons with her. Dayna looked back and laughed. Other groups backstage that I hadn't even noticed started laughing too. There I stood, all alone, feeling like I'd been bitten with venom and was left there for my dreams to die.

***

I couldn't believe this. Just when I thought I found a group that I fit in with—maybe not perfectly, but at least fit into—it was too good to be true. They were about to take the stage, and I wasn't going on there with them. How were they going to adjust? When I heard their first note, the harmony with three sounded fine. They were showing me they didn't need me at all, so I needed to get the heck out of there, and that's what I did. I couldn't get out of the theater because Avery stood in my way.

"Wait, wait, wait, let's talk, beautiful," he placed his arm on my shoulders and said.

"Are you serious? You're calling me beautiful, and my group just dropped me because of you," I said, smacking his hand away.

"Did you not mean the things you said? Forget them, they're just jealous."

Huffing and puffing, I said, "Why would you think I want to be with someone who just broke my friend's heart? If you made her all crazy, I'm not going to give you the chance to make me the same way. Move out of my way."

"You need to let me explain before you just accuse me of whatever she told you. There're two sides to every story last time I checked. Taylor Dale is a stalker. I mean, shucks, she was smothering me. I couldn't take it. A girl looks my way, and she's trying to fight her. I don't call her every hour, and she's crying. So I cut her loose. I wasn't rude, mean, or harsh to her, but there was no way to say it to somebody who honestly wasn't mentally all there. I mean dang, she acted like she owned me. Nobody should be in a relationship like that."

I rolled my eyes and looked up at the ceiling. I heard what he was saying, but it just wasn't adding up. I mean, he was right. There were two sides to every story. How could I tell if his side was the right one? I did witness firsthand that he broke Taylor's heart, and I wasn't trying to break it all over again.

"Come here, girl," he said as he grabbed me and then kissed me like somebody out of a movie would.

First it was feeling good. Heck, I never had been kissed before. I didn't know what I was doing. But I didn't ask for the kiss either, so I stepped back and slapped him as hard as I could.

"Hey! What's going on here?" I heard Shelby ask.

"Yeah, what are you doing to my sister?" Sloan demanded, with all my sisters by her side.

"You need to step back," Shelby said to him.

He put his hands in the air. "Sorry."

"What's the problem here?" Sloan asked me.

Shaking my head, I said, "It's a whole long story."

"We didn't hear you sing. Isn't that your group up on stage?" Yuri asked, trying to move past the drama they walked in on.

"You just hit this guy. You're supposed to be on stage with those girls. Something happened. You need to tell us now before we call the police," Shelby said. "Is he messing with you?"

"I've got this, y'all. Just please, please leave," I said to my sisters.

"We're not leaving you alone with some guy you just slapped. Obviously he was out of line or you wouldn't have done that," Shelby told me as her eyes locked on mine.

"You're still here?" Dayna came up to me and said. "We kicked you out. I thought you'd be gone by now."

"Kicked her out of what?" Shelby asked.

"I'll explain to y'all at home. Let's go," I uttered, grabbing Sloan's hand, since she was standing near me, to leave.

"Yeah, you better take your sisters and leave," Dayna called out.

"Excuse me?" Sloan turned around and said.

Fed up and pissed, I said, "Y'all just go on to the car. Let me handle this witch."

"Handle me? Whatever," Dayna grunted, almost spitting on me.

Wiping off the mist from my cheek, I said, "You the one who set this whole thing up! You knew Avery was the guy I was talking about."

"I didn't know anything. Don't try to put words in my mouth," Dayna lashed back.

I said, "Oh, so you're going to deny it. You can't even woman up and admit that you set this whole thing up, knowing he was the same guy that had just broken up with Taylor!"

"So you like this guy?" Sloan asked.

"Please, Sloan. I told you I would explain this later."

Dayna laughed. "You need to talk to your sister now because you all up in my face working your neck, you'll get it broken off."

"I dare you to touch me. You're all talk, but you ain't got no backbone," I said to Dayna.

She pushed me, and I pushed her back. She pushed me again, and I pushed her back. The next thing you know, the two of us were on the ground tussling, someone from another group waiting to perform was recording it. It was a mess. Two of my sisters grabbed me.

I yelled out, "Naw, let me shut her up."

Shelby and Ansli pulled me up. Sloan grabbed my bag that had my costume and everything in it. Yuri looked over at me with scratches all on my face, and she shook her head. As we were about to head out, the contestants were being called back on stage. I didn't turn back, but the crowd erupted when Avery's name was called.

"Keep it moving, sis." Shelby pushed me in the back and said.

In the car, Sloan said, "What in the world, Slade? People got that mess on tape."

I uttered, "So what? I was supposed to sit there and let her push me? Let her talk to me any ol' kind of way?"

"No, you did what you had to do. I'm just sorry it didn't work out for you," Yuri said. "I know you really wanted to be in a group."

"I did, but girls are a trip. I guess I just wanted what you guys have so bad."

"What do you mean 'have what we have'?" Ansli asked.

Tears were starting to well up in my eyes as if someone had turned on a faucet.

"You guys always pair up. I'm always the odd man out."

"You're always with me and Yuri," Sloan said, clearly not understanding what I was talking about.

I said, "I just don't have a best friend, okay? But I guess I'm learning it ain't nothing wrong with having my sisters. At least it's real. I got to settle for the fact that maybe my dream is not gonna ever come true."

"Now you're talking silly," Ansli said. "You're way more talented than me, and if I could make something of my dream then you could do the same. But you've got to be with the right people."

Knowing she was right and that I was with the right people I uttered, "I don't want to go home right now, you guys."

"Well let's go get a big, fat burger and some fries," Yuri said, feeling me.

I smiled and nodded. I was truly thankful for my sisters. The five of us gulped down big juicy burgers with cheese, and during my time with them, I forgot my woes. Eventually, we had to head to the Sharp estate.

As soon as we walked into the house, our parents were sitting there waiting on us—and not because they didn't know where we were. Ansli made sure we checked in. The fight had gone viral. The headline was, "How can Sharp run the city when he can't even control his daughters?" It was just me fighting, but the video made it seem like all of us were out of control.

"Explain this. Somebody tell me what's going on here," my dad said as he held up his iPad.

"Somebody stepped to Slade wrong, Dad," Yuri said.

"Yeah, but sweetheart, you can't just fight," my father responded in a sweet tone.

I stepped up and took responsibility. "I wasn't trying to ruin your campaign, Dad, and I hope I didn't do that, but . . ."

"But what?" my mom asked. "You just begged me to spend the night with these girls. You were in a group with them, and now you're fighting one of them. What in the world happened?"

"Jealousy," Shelby uttered.

"Well listen, that doesn't surprise me at all," my dad said, surprising me. "But you've got to be bigger than that, Slade Angel Sharp. Somebody steps to you wanting to fight, you've got to step back. The stakes are real high."

"But it ain't cool to punk out, Dad," I voiced.

"It ain't cool to get a juvenile record either, Slade. And whether I'm the mayor or not, this family is already on front street. I know that's a lot of pressure you girls didn't ask for, but if ever there were five young ladies who could rise to the occasion, it's my girls. Don't let anybody change you from who you are. Slade Sharp doesn't slither on the ground attacking people. That's somebody else's M.O., ya feel?" he said.

He patted my head and took my mom by the arm and walked out. He turned back to me and gave me a wink.

***

A week had gone by, and I couldn't get Avery out of my mind. He was in my dreams and my thoughts, and when I came out of the school building, he was in my reality. Or was my mind just playing tricks on me again? I blinked several times, and there he was actually standing there waving at me.

The election was getting closer, and my sisters all went with Shelby to go to my dad's campaign headquarters. I was going home. I had a project coming up, and thanks to Ansli being on punishment because she skipped school, I had been driving her car. My dad understood that I couldn't help because of my school work. Though I had to get my project done, Avery's presence put it on the back burner. My sister Sloan would never be diverted from get her work done. My name wasn't Sloan, though.

Getting close to him, I put on a poker face. I had to ignore him. He was toxic.

"You just gon' ignore me? You see me waving. You not saying anything. You still that mad at me? Come on, I thought you'd be over it by now," he said.

He was so fine, I wanted to pass out. I held it together, though. He couldn't see me sweat.

"Avery, why are you here at Marks High?" I said when I touched his shoulder. I actually felt chills go through my body when I felt a muscle. "Are you getting back with Taylor or something?"

"No, I'm here because I need you." Avery was looking deeply into my eyes.

"Excuse me?" I said, moving back from him.

"No, no, really. I mean don't get me wrong. I'd love to have the opportunity to win you over, but I really need your help."

"With what?" I asked.

"I've got to cut this demo for a friend. Your voice . . . I need you for background. I promise it won't take too long."

My dad had spies everywhere, even in the form of the principal, so if I was going to do something daring, I had to get to it. Not totally thinking through what I was agreeing to, I just said yes.

"Great! You can ride with me, and just leave your car here."

"Uh, no," I told him, with a big attitude and a frown. "I'll follow you."

"Alright," Avery said, seeing I was serious. "I appreciate this. Really. You'll be there an hour tops."

"That's all I have because I got to get home. I've got a big project due tomorrow, and my parents are expecting me to be home when they arrive."

"Thank you," he said, stroking my hand.

It took us about fifteen minutes to get to a house. I actually thought we were going to a studio, but as we were walking up to the door, Avery told me the studio was in a back room. When we arrived at the eerie house, I felt a little uncomfortable. I saw nothing but guys. And not young ones either. They all looked to be twenty and older. There were even more of them inside the house. I started coughing when smoke hit my lungs, but it wasn't smoke from cigarettes or even cigars. These jokers were smoking weed.

"Where are you taking me?" I said to him, getting really agitated.

Before he could answer, the Boots guy from backstage at the pageant stepped up to him. "You're late."

"I know. I'm sorry, Boots," Avery said to him.

"Get in there and make my hit record. K.J. is already in there."

I was pissed when I found out we were here because Avery was trying to pay off some of the debt he owed. "Avery, I'm not staying."

I turned around to walk out. He grabbed my waist, pulled me to him, looked me eye-to-eye, and said, "Please. I know this seems crazy, me bringing you here like this. But if I didn't need you, I wouldn't have."

Then all I could do was flash back to the night he was getting punched in the gut, and I said, "Alright. Hurry up."

Avery opened the door, and we started a session. I sat on the couch when he recorded the lead vocal tracks. Without fail, hearing his voice again made me want to take off my clothes and let him do all the things he was singing about.

When it was my time to add the chorus, my creative juices kicked in. And when he told me what he wanted me to sing, I asked him, "How 'bout this?" and tried something way sexier. He loved it.

"Record it. I'll be right back," he told me when there was a knock on the door.

"Hey, sexy lady. You ready to start?"

I couldn't see who was on the other side of the engineering booth.

"Yeah, I guess."

"One, two, a one, two, three, go."

I sang. Before I knew it, a guy appeared before me, and he was about two hundred and fifty pounds, with a little gut that I could see. It was October, but he had on a cut-off T-shirt. He looked nasty, and he kept walking toward me.

"Shucks, you fine. Come touch Daddy," he said with his gross lips.

"What?" I said, falling on the couch as I was backing up. He fell on top of me. "Get off of me!"

This K.J. guy covered my mouth and started touching my chest. I couldn't even move. This guy was trying to rape me. His lower body was slithering on me like a snake.

CHAPTER FIVE
STRETCH

K.J.'s gritty dog-hands were all over my waist. His funky, nasty breath was all in my face. When slobber fell from his mouth and onto my lips, I felt more uncomfortable than I ever had in my life.

"Stop!" I screamed out. "Don't do this!"

"Just ease up baby, dang. It's ain't going to take long," K.J. said as his rough, sticky hands went to my jeans.

I was happy they were tight. It made it difficult for him to unbutton them and pull them down. As hard as I tried to wiggle away, he controlled my movement.

"Please get off of me! Please," I yelled when he touched my skin down low.

He was digging deep, trying to find my treasure. I was moving erratically, trying not to give him a map. Just as he got inches from a hot spot, the creep was pulled off of me. I was too afraid to sit up.

Then I heard Avery punching him and saying, "You have no business touching her."

I sat up quickly and buttoned my pants. I screamed, "Avery, let's just go! Come on! Let's go!"

When Avery looked up at me, K.J. got the upper hand. The jerk put Avery in a chokehold. He would not let up.

As he squeezed Avery tighter, I screamed, "Help! Somebody help!"

I didn't know where we were, and I didn't know whose house we were in, but surely there had to be decent people who weren't for all this violence. Thankfully three guys rushed in and pulled K.J. off of Avery. When they stood together, I was real creeped out because Boots was in the middle. It was déjà vu seeing the same guys who had threatened Avery before at his mom's theater looking to do the same thing again. I knew he owed Boots dough, but was being here worth it?

Boots grabbed Avery's arm and said, "I ain't want no trouble. You just was supposed to come in here and make me a hit record, paying back some of what you owe. I liked the sound you just played, but now you want to come over here bringing this chick who doesn't understand the game. We take what we want in my house."

"She didn't come here for that, Boots," Avery said.

Boots grabbed Avery's collar. "I wasn't asking you all that. I said we get what we want in my house, so get her out of here, and just know now we're back to zero. You owe me all my money. I want it in two weeks, or I'm going to let my partners here finish what they started with you and your mom. You hear me? Two weeks!"

Avery nodded and grabbed my hand. I reached back down to grab my purse, and the two of us fled like we just stole something.

As soon as we got outside he said, "I know you drove, but just follow me, please. I want to explain. Just follow me.

"I—I got to go home," I said, still shaking.

"Just please follow me."

Still worried about Avery, I told him I would. He walked me to my car. When I saw thugs eyeing me down, instinctively I marked the location using the GPS.

We went to a park. I pulled up right beside him. Avery motioned for me to come over to his car. Against my better judgment, I went and got into his car.

"It's getting late, I can't stay long," I said to him.

"I know," he said as he stroked my hair. "I just want to make sure you're okay."

"No, I'm not okay. I'm shaking from top to bottom. Why did you take me there? Those are the same guys who threatened you and your mom."

"You know I was trying to pay down some of the debt."

"Okay, but why did you take me there? They

are crazy as I don't know what, and as soon as you left, he tried to *rape* me."

"Of course I didn't know that he was going to do that."

"What if he would have killed you? None of this is worth it. We just have to try to find the money so you can pay him and be done with it. You can't deal with those guys again," I stated with intense emotion.

"I will handle it. I just need you to calm down."

"How can I calm down? I was almost raped tonight," I uttered hysterically as I relived the horrific moment.

"I'm sorry about that. I don't know what I would have done if something would have happened to you," he said, sounding equally upset.

"Thank you for coming in and getting him off of me. He's two times your size, and he was there one minute and gone the next," I said.

"Seeing someone hurting you just gave me extra strength."

Really needing to understand, I asked, "Why did you get mixed up with them in the first place?"

"I don't want to talk about this, Slade. I just want to show you I'm sorry. I just want to erase away the memories of somebody touching you with such force. I want to make you feel good. Can I kiss you?"

Spellbound I guess, I nodded. His lips touched mine, and it was the exact opposite of the feeling I felt an hour ago. This time I felt liberated as his hands roamed around my chest and all over my back. He stopped just before I had to say, "I'm not ready for anything else." I certainly could understand why Taylor was so crazy about him. This guy had it going on, and he was a gentleman. I didn't think I was ready to be intimate with a guy, but he probably could pull me in a direction I didn't think I was ready to go. His hands were just that magical, but after the last kiss, he changed it to business.

"You're talented, you know. I left the studio because I had to go share with the other guys how cool the sound was. Don't let Taylor and those girls stop you. If you want to get a group . . . create one."

"How can I get a group?"

"Well, if want to go solo, then you do that."

"I like being in a group, though."

Touching my brow with concern in his fingertips, he said, "I'm just saying don't let the dream stop. You're better than all three of them, and I know a producer. If you want to cut a record we could do that."

"I'm not going back to that house."

"No, I don't mean them. They got whack equipment. Maybe you can scrape up a few dollars and book some studio time at a real place. I'm just saying when you're ready, I'm here."

And then we leaned back and enjoyed the stars. When I looked at my watch, I realized I needed to get home. Avery gave me something to think about, a whole bunch of things actually, and all of them were positive.

***

October was flying by. I had been so busy with my family doing so many appearances and getting ready for the upcoming election. I'd been trying to help my father win so much that I hadn't seen Taylor and her girls. That was just fine with me 'cause when I looked up, they were staring at me, and they saw me looking at them. All three sets of eyes stared really hard.

"Whatever," I said to myself now that I knew I was truly attracted to Avery, even though I hadn't talked to him in a week.

He and I had a connection that I wasn't willing to give up for her. So it was just best she stayed with her little group and I stayed on my own. No need to beg her for a friendship.

Later that day, it was lunch time. I was walking to get my food, and I got a text from Charlotte, who was in the pageant.

It read, "Hey, I see you. Wanna have lunch?"

"Sure," I texted back. "But I don't see you."

"Just sit there at that table. I'm getting my food now," Charlotte texted.

"K," I texted back.

The bubbly blonde came and sat right beside me. "How have you been? I've been looking for you. I know we go to the same school, but I was sick with bronchitis, so I stayed away for a couple weeks."

"I'm not trying to get sick," I said, moving away a bit.

She laughed. "I'm fully better now, or I wouldn't be here. I'm glad I saw you today. We've got to hang out."

"How's it been being Miss Teen Charlotte, Charlotte?" I asked, really wanting to know.

"Fun. It's still not what I really want to do. Going around meeting people, taking pictures, shaking hands . . ."

Cutting her off, I asked, "Well, what do you want to do?"

Then she started humming, and I remembered her voice was angelic. I immediately thought hers coupled with mine would make a dynamic group. Ebony and Ivory. Not that that's what we would call ourselves, but we'd definitely stand out. People would underestimate us until they heard our sound.

"Let me ask you this question. Would you have time to sing with me? And not just for fun, like seriously. Maybe seeing if we got some kind of vibe to form a group or something?"

"Oh my gosh! I would love that," she said,

getting all excited.

She reached over and hugged me.

"Are you serious? You'd be okay with that?" I questioned as her enthusiasm seemed too good to be true.

"Yes, Slade, I'd love to. Being Miss Teen Charlotte is a means to an end. I want to sing. Sometimes people just see a white girl, but I got some soul in me. If I partnered with you, the sky would be the limit."

Smiling and happy, I said, "When are we going to practice?"

"I could come over later today."

"I don't know about today. I always have to check with my parents to see what they have for me."

"Alright, let me know," Charlotte said.

"Will do." I was tickled pink, realizing I had just formed a group.

We finished our food. As I was about to head to class, I got another text. When I looked down, I knew it was from Taylor.

"If you don't mind, could you meet me in the bathroom? I really need to talk to you."

"No," I quickly texted back. "I'm not meeting you in anybody's bathroom."

The only thing I could think about is that she wanted to have her girls beat me up, corner me or something. I wasn't falling for that. Absolutely not.

Taylor texted, "Okay, okay, can you just stay right there? I really do need to talk to you."

"About what?" I texted back.

"It's important."

So I waited. Pretty much everybody was leaving lunch. I sat still, waiting on Taylor's tail.

When I was about to forget her and get going, Dr. Garner came over and said, "Ms. Sharp, aren't you supposed to be heading back to class?"

"I'm walking right now, sir. I was waiting on Taylor Dale. There she is," I explained as Taylor walked up. "She had to put away her tray."

"Oh, alright. You girls get on to class," Dr. Garner told us.

"Thanks for waiting," Taylor said, trying to ease the irritation on my brow.

"You're about to get me in trouble. What's

this about? Or is that the intention?" I said, truly not trusting her.

"No, no . . . first of all, I owe you an apology."

"Oh, you're going to apologize to me?" I said sarcastically. "You kick me out of your group after assuming I knew Avery was your man."

I really didn't want to go down that road with her because, now, I *did* know that was her ex, and I wanted him for myself. I mean I wanted her man before, but I just didn't know it was her man. Yeah, that's a place I didn't want to go.

"Forget that. You were right. He wasn't into me. I needed to let him go," Taylor admitted, surprising me with her response.

"I'm not coming back to the group. I'm doing my own thing," I said to her, not sure what she was up to, but sure I needed to set her straight right away.

I didn't even have my group with Charlotte solidified, but I wasn't trying to be back with those tricks anymore. They weren't going to sit me in the fool's chair and have me recline. Besides, I wasn't gonna let them get my hopes up just to dash them away.

"No, this isn't about the group," Taylor uttered loud and clear. "My mom, she's got this thing after school for kids who are in a low socio-economic group, and I need to bring somebody to help me mentor them. She told me a long time ago. I mentioned it to Dayna and Caylen, but . . ."

"But your friends don't want to give back to the community. I'm not surprised."

Not wanting to admit her friends were trifling, she explained, "They've got something else to do."

"Yeah, okay."

"So, I just wonder . . ."

"What? You want to use me?"

"You seemed really into the class when we were there last time. My mom doesn't know we fell out, and she actually requested you. If you say no, I understand," she said as she started walking away. "I'll figure something out."

"Wait, wait, it's just an hour after school?"

"Yeah."

"For your mom and the kids, I'll do it," I told her, even though she had hurt me bad.

Still skeptical, I followed her over to her mom's elementary music class. It was like I was in a whole different world. Those little kids were adorable. They didn't have the best clothes, and their hair was a little mangled. You could tell they didn't have much, but they had great spirits, and they were fired up to sing. As I was playing with them, they blossomed even more, appreciating the time. Then, at the end, Taylor's mom told them that the sessions were going to be ending soon. This was a paid after-school music program, and the funds were going to be cut.

The little kids squealed in a chorus, "No!"

My heart broke. When I saw Taylor crying, I knew she had a heart, too. I got it. Many of these kids didn't have any other place to go. This program provided so much. They got a snack in the afternoon. Without this program, a lot of them wouldn't be fed until they got back to school the next day. This program couldn't go away, but when I realized I had no way to help, I became depressed, and I started singing "My Favorite Things" from *The Sound of Music*.

Doing so, at least I put a smile back on the kids' faces as well as on mine, even if it was only for the here and now.

***

"So you and the queen are going to be a group?" Shelby asked when Charlotte came over to our house to practice.

I hit my sister in the side. She was playing, but she was serious. Shelby had doubts about how Charlotte and I would sound.

"Just hold on," I told my doubting sister.

When the two of us started singing, all four of my sisters' mouths hung open.

"Oh, you guys need to be doing this," Sloan uttered as she clapped.

"Yeah, you two sound really good," Yuri said.

"I'm ready to take some pictures," Ansli commented.

"My bad," Shelby looked at me and said. "I stand corrected. You all sound great. We've got to get you guys the entire package: a name, a look, and a demo."

"I know a guy who can help us with that," I said to Charlotte.

"You let me know. I'm ready. Send me over the track you were talking about, and I will practice it," Charlotte said.

She was so easy to work with. She wasn't trying to out-sing me. She just wanted to be a part of it.

When my sisters left, Charlotte and I had to talk business. I asked, "How are we going to do this?"

"I just want to be an artist. I don't want to be a part of the business side."

"Well, I'll ask my dad for some money to cut the record, but that'll mean I'll own more of it. Is that cool?" I questioned, knowing these tough negotiations needed to be addressed.

"Absolutely. You got all this help with all your sisters to do a record label."

"Oh, you're taking it a little too far," I told her, knowing I just wanted to cut a demo.

"No. If we're going to do this, we need to step it up, for real," Charlotte encouraged. "Create a label."

"Alright, well, I've got to talk to my dad, and I'll get back to you, but I like the direction we're going. We should come up with a name, though."

"You'll come up with one," she said.

"You're really letting me do all the creative work?"

"Yeah, and I'm a performer. I merely sing what I'm told and show up when I'm supposed to perform. You on the other hand are a double threat. You can sing, and you can be behind the scenes, so don't limit yourself. Plus, I have all this Miss Teen Charlotte stuff with me, and I'm not trying to rub it in or anything . . ."

"No, no, no, you're right. You do that, and I can come up with the business side of our group, and we can sing together. I love it!"

"Well, at least just promise me this . . . no matter what happens, we'll stay friends. I know we don't really, really know each other," Charlotte said. "But you have to come hang out at my house too. My folks have to get to know you."

We shook on it. Being with Charlotte was going to be worry free. I felt bad that I hated on her when she beat me out. Getting to know her, it was clear that she deserved it.

Two days passed, and I hadn't had the chance to talk to my dad about my dreams. Both of my older two sisters were already operating in their gifts. The fashion designer extraordinaire, Shelby Sharp, was trying to come up with the look for my group that I didn't even have a name for. Ansli couldn't wait to take photos of us for the CD that I didn't even have.

I needed to get on the ball. I needed to talk to my dad about a loan. Though I knew he was in the middle of trying to run a big race, he always said his daughters came first. Now it was time for him to be real about that and take time out for his daughter. I wasn't going to feel bad about that. I needed my father to believe in me and invest in the group, so I knocked on his office door.

He looked up and said, "Slade! Come in, babe."

"I know you're busy."

"Not too busy for you. What's up?"

"I love you, Daddy!" I said as I hugged his

neck real tight.

"How much money do you want, and for what do you want it?"

"Dad . . ."

"Don't 'Dad' me. I know you girls. Your mom has trained you well," he teased.

I just laughed. I went from behind his desk to sit in front of him in the chair. He needed to view me professionally.

"Can we talk business?"

"My creative daughter wants to talk business? Okay. What's up? You have my full attention."

"I think I want to start a record label. Well, I'm not sure if I want to start a record label, but I at least want to have some money to start producing my own record."

"And what do you know about all of this? How much is it going to cost? How you are going to make money back?" my father drilled me.

He asked me those questions and many more. I kind of just looked at him like, 'Why are you getting that deep? Just give me the money already.'

He said, "I'll tell you what. After school tomorrow, we're going to make a few stops. Once you talk to the people I want you to talk to, if you still want to do this, then we can push forward."

"Alright," I said a little frustrated and confused.

Before I left out of his office he got up and grabbed my hand, "Trust me. You want to be prepared. It's not just about having a passion. If you really want to pursue a dream, this isn't going to be painless."

"Yes, sir," I said.

***

Sure enough after school, I came straight home. He was waiting for me. We took off. First stop: a place where cash overflows. When we actually went to the bank, I smiled so hard my smile stretched from the bank to our house. He was going to give me the money. We sat right down with the owner of the bank.

"My daughter wants some money to cut a record. She said she might want to start a business plan. Mr. Martin, could you talk to her? Should I give her the money?" My smile faded.

"First of all, how much money is she talking about?" Mr. Martin asked.

Gritting my teeth, I said, "Well, I haven't exactly figured that out. Whatever he starts me out with is fine."

Mr. Martin showed no mercy. "What if it is not enough? Then you're going to come back and ask for more. We're supposed to just keep giving you more? Here's how it works here at the bank. When people come here trying to get a loan, usually they show us a business plan and show us not only how much money they're asking for, but also a plan on how they're going to spend the money and how they plan on making money back. If you're serious about what you're doing, then you need to show your dad a business plan. I'm recommending he sees it before he gives you a dime."

The two of them talked small talk for a little while longer, and I had to sit there thinking through my business plan for a company that had just popped into my head. All I wanted was the money, and now I had to think deeper. That was frustrating.

Our next stop: the other side of the tracks. I wouldn't call it the ghetto, but it looked close to the projects. My dad wasn't turning back, so I guess I was in for another lesson.

"Dad, where are we going?" I asked.

When we pulled up at a trailer, he asked, "Do you remember the song, 'Shake it, Break it'?"

"No."

"Well, it was a hot song. YouTube it. M.C. Nails is the artist."

That name sounded familiar. "Yeah, I think I remember him."

My dad got out the car and motioned for me to follow. M.C. Nails greeted us at the door. My dad must have told him who I was.

"Nice to meet you, young lady. I just want to tell you if you're going to go into the record business, you need to be a smart business woman. I made so much money off of my first song, and then stupid me blew it all. The record business is more than just about the sound and the glitz and the glamour. It's also about dollars and cents. If you're going to go into it, be wise so you won't end up like me with nothing."

He and my dad also talked a little business, and then we were off again. Last stop: Mundy Records. I couldn't believe I was sitting in Mr. Mundy's office. I just sat with him a couple weeks ago when he was at my school.

He said, "You want to have a record company? Well, I'm trying hard to keep my head above water. It's not an easy business to be in. I'm always trying to get the next hottest and greatest artist out there. Be sure you're ready."

I responded, "Well, I just want to make one album, sir. I wasn't fortunate enough to win your competition, so I'm just trying to make my own way. I can't believe my dad knows you."

"Yeah, we go way back, and I'd love to mentor you along the way. Though I've got to be honest, Stanley," Mr. Mundy said to my dad, "I don't even know if I'm going to be able to keep my doors open, so helping your daughter right about now is a stretch."

CHAPTER SIX
SCHEME

"So you still thinking about my kiss?" Avery seductively said to me on the phone.

Holding the phone between my shoulder and my ear, I looked up at the ceiling and had my hands raised. I don't know if I was trying to imagine him on top of me or if I was going crazy. Just talking to the guy had me spinning.

He purred, "You're not answering me, and you know I'm dying to see you again. My lips are dry. When can we connect?"

"It hasn't even been a week, and the last time I was with you I got in a whole bunch of trouble."

"Wait, straight up, I'm being serious now," Avery changed his tone and said. "Please tell me you hadn't been thinking about those guys. Again, I'm sorry. K.J. had no right to force himself on you like that."

"No, no, no. You came in just in the nick of time. I don't have nightmares or anything, and you did a pretty good job of helping me forget the events of that day. When I think back on it, I'm definitely not thinking about him. I got in trouble with you."

He let out a sweet sigh. "When can we see each other?"

"Well, you're not going to be the one to ask all the questions."

"Okay, what do you want to know?"

"Have you settled everything with those goons?"

"Goons . . . that's a weird word."

"Okay, creeps, jerks, hoodlums, guys that have no problem roughing up you, me, or your mom."

Huffing, he sighed, "Okay I get ya. I got that. You don't need to worry about it."

"So that's a yes?"

"Tell me about your business. You're going to start the record label? We gonna cut a demo? Did you and that queen form a group or what?"

"You're changing the subject, Avery," I stated, a bit agitated.

"That's cuz I don't want you stressed, Slade," he uttered back in his sultry and enticing voice.

"I like the way you say my name," I said to him, getting myself off track.

Avery was a dream. He was so daggone hot that even through a phone his voice sent chills up my spine. I didn't even realize I was squirming in the bed and biting the blanket until the door abruptly opened.

My mother shouted, "Slade, what in the world are you doing?"

"Okay, I got to go," I rolled over and said, as I quickly hung up on Avery, unable to even fathom an explanation that would make sense.

Irritated, she huffed, "What were you doing feeling all over yourself like you done lost your mind?"

I guess I had lost my mind. I didn't know if

it was the porn, if it was the kiss, if it was just me growing or what, but I wasn't the same old sweet, innocent Slade anymore. Maybe some of the sexy music I was singing was making my hormones go crazy. Whatever it was, I had changed.

My mom and I had always been cool, so I sat up and said, "Can we talk?"

The way I said it let her know that I was serious. If she didn't want to know what was going on with me, then she needed to just say no because she wasn't ready to hear that her little girls were growing up. I couldn't speak for Shelby, Ansli, Sloan, or Yuri, but I for sure could speak for Slade. I really did need a cool mom to talk to about it all. She came over and sat beside me.

She took my hand, looked me square in the eye, and said, "Yes, for sure. You know it. You can talk to me. What's up?"

"It's this guy."

Half joking, she gasped, "Not you too . . . are you serious? What is going on with you girls? You were playing with Barbies, and now you all want to play with Ken?"

"Ha, ha, ha, Mom."

"No, I'm really serious. Who is this boy? Where'd you meet him, and how serious is it? I send you girls to public school, and all of y'all lose your mind. Only wanting to study anatomy or something."

"Whatever, Mom," I teased and nudged her. "Girls in private school are having sex too."

"So you're having sex?" she snapped.

"Mom, I didn't say that! But I mean, if you're going to trip like this, then forget it."

She got up and paced the floor for a minute, holding her head like she had a headache. I hadn't even really told her anything. I guess all the stuff she was imagining had her stressed.

"When did you lose your virginity?" I asked her, really wanting to know.

"Slade Sharp, don't make this about me."

"So it was young then, huh?"

"I didn't say that."

"Yeah, but you didn't say it wasn't. If it was a time frame that you thought was appropriate, you would be the first to blab it. Since you're holding it back, I know that means you don't

117

want me to have information I could use against you. That's lawyer thinking," I smiled and said.

"And you'd make a good one, it seems." My mom scratched her head and took a deep sigh. "I made some choices that I'm not proud of. I made some mistakes I don't want you to repeat. I wish I would have waited. But can I live your life? No. Can I throw you in a convent and do away with the key? As your parent, I probably have that right, but what good would it do you? I want you to grow. I want you to make your own mistakes. Most importantly, Slade honey, I want you to be the smart young lady that I raised you to be. You got this company we were supposed to work on tomorrow. I got a lot of things lined up for you to get your ducks in a row. The last thing I want you thinking about is spreading your legs for some guy. I mean, what I just saw you doing on this bed, are you practicing or what?"

Embarrassed, I softly voiced, "I don't know, Mom. I wish I could explain what's going on with me. This guy, he's so hot, and he's seeping into my dreams."

"Tell me he's in school."

"Yes ma'am. He's a junior this year like me. He just doesn't go to Marks but another school in the city."

"And his grades?"

I didn't really know, but I didn't want her worried, so it took me a second to answer. "Good."

"You hesitated. Do you know what his grades are?" She's really good at her dang job.

"No, no, no, they're good. I mean, he wants to be a producer and singer like me."

Throwing her hands up, she said, "Oh, that's just great. Don't you guys know that's a hard career to get into?"

"Yeah, Mom, but it's very lucrative, and we've got to chase our dreams. You followed yours, right?" I rationalized.

With a grim face, she took my hand and asked, "Honey, do I need to get you on birth control pills?"

"I don't think right now."

"You don't think?"

"Okay, not right now."

"But you promise me, if things change, you'll tell me? And don't tell your father. My goodness, he'll probably jump off a cliff," she tried joking.

"We're growing up, Mom."

"I know, baby," she said as she hugged me. "And we've got to start having more talks like this because I've got girls, and I'm not trying to be a grandmother. Be ready early in the morning. Sharp Records . . . that's what your mind needs to be focused on."

"But you aren't all for it," I said, knowing deep down she wished I had a different passion.

"Well, trust me. A record company or a guy . . . your Sharp Records dream will win out every time in my view."

***

The next morning she kept her promise. We were up early. We went to the Secretary of State's office and filed for a tax ID number. Since I wasn't old enough, my mom had to put down her information too. We filed for a trademark, and she showed me several business plans. We chose one that wasn't too cumbersome, and she had me sit down all day to put in my thoughts of what I wanted. I had to research companies that could make the DVDs for me at a minimal price but with good quality. Once all that was done and I had a great plan, she helped me present it to my father. I walked him through every aspect of what Sharp Records was planning to do, and he smiled. After that, my parents took me to open a bank account. I got a one thousand dollar loan to start my business. When I saw the balance in the account, my mom smiled and pinched my cheeks. I know what she was thinking. "See, look at you all proud of yourself. You put your mind into business, and you weren't even thinking about that boy." And she was right. But I couldn't wait to tell Avery. So maybe she was wrong because he wasn't that far off my mind.

***

"Hey, Slade. When we going to the studio?" Charlotte asked me later that day, for the fourth day in a row.

"I don't know. I've been trying to get in touch with Avery, but he hasn't called me back. This is so unlike him."

"Yeah, that's your boo, right?" Charlotte teased.

"I don't know about all that, but I definitely thought he liked me, Charlotte. Now he's not even returning my calls. I'm trying to give him some work . . . I don't know. Just seems a little shady," I voiced in an irritated tone.

Calmly she asked, "Do you know where he lives?"

"I don't, but I know where his mom works."

"Duh, if you're really concerned, you need to head over there."

When we hung up the phone, I knew Charlotte was right. What she didn't know that I knew was that Avery was mixed up with some salty jokers. It had been days since I tried to get him. The fact that he hadn't called me back was extremely alarming. I just couldn't sit back and pray that everything would be okay. I had to put some action behind what I was thinking and investigate.

I had to be smart about this. I had gotten out the house without worrying my family. They thought I was just going to the mall to find a cute outfit for the photo shoot, but I drove straight to the theater.

A car was around back. I hoped it belonged to his mother. I didn't want to alarm her. I needed to be careful to make sure that I just asked for Avery. If he was alright and just had a change of heart about wanting to pursue a relationship with me, then I needed to deal with that. I could be a big girl and move on if need be. I had given Taylor that same talk, and I was not above taking in the good advice. I had too much self-esteem to even be thinking about chasing down a brother, but I did need closure.

When I got inside, I found his mom pacing back and forth in the same office where I had seen her earlier in the month. She was also shaking. Before I could speak to her, she started dialing the phone.

She cried out, "Avery, son, why didn't you come home last night? Please call me. I'm going out of my mind."

At that moment, it was confirmed I did have something to worry about. I felt sick to my stomach, like I had been poisoned. Now I was shaking.

"Ms. Hardy," I said as I stepped into view.

"Yes, may I help you?"

I hesitated. "I'm, I'm friends with your son."

"You know where he is?" she asked.

"Well, I wasn't trying to be nosy, but it appears he's missing."

"I know that. I'm asking if you know where he is . . . wait," she said as she squinted my way, "Where do I know you from?"

"At the pageant. I was the one that was back here," I told her, not trying to spend much time on the past as we needed every second to find Avery.

"Oh my gosh, you sure were. You were listening in that day, and it seems like you're listening in now."

"Because I'm concerned about your son, and I didn't want to alarm you or tell . . ." I cut myself off, not wanting to speculate that Boots had him.

"What do you know? Just spit it out. I haven't seen him all night! What do you know?" she drilled.

Taking a deep breath, I said, "I don't know for sure, but I was working with him on a demo, and we went to some house, and the guys there were the same guys who said he owed them money that day."

"Where's this house?" she asked in a panic.

Thinking back I said, "I put the location in the GPS when I left, so it's in my car."

"Great, I'll follow you," Ms. Hardy said as she went to grab her purse and coat.

I cautioned, "It's not the kind of place we want to show up just you and me."

Exhaling she said, "My friend is a cop. You stand right there, I'm going to call him."

While I didn't think I needed to pray earlier, now that I truly believed Avery was at that house, prayer was the only thing that could help him. Those guys were crazy, and they had it in for him. If he didn't have their money, it might already be too late.

"Sam! You've got to meet me at this house.

This friend of Avery's thinks she knows where he is . . . No, no, I'm going to leave now. I can't sit here and wait," his mom said.

"We should wait," I said, reemphasizing that I didn't want the two of us to go there without backup.

His mom might be all big and bad. However, seeing that I remembered her being restrained as the same guys were roughly handling her, she should know we were no match for them alone. I wasn't moving without real backup.

"Okay, okay," she said to me. Then she talked back into the receiver. "Hurry up, Sam."

She hung up the phone. "He said he'll be here in ten minutes, and then we can follow you. I can't believe my son was taking you to these guys' house."

I wanted to tell her it wasn't a great experience, but she was already worried enough. The fifteen minutes we had to wait for Sam to show up seemed like an hour, but finally he arrived. He wanted me to give him the address, but Ms. Hardy said we'd already wasted too much time waiting for him. He explained that they would be right behind me and once we got to the house I didn't need to park close.

When I got in my car, I programed the GPS to take me to the previous destination. I realized this was serious, and my dad deserved to know where I was going. On the way I called him.

"Hey, pumpkin. Your mom told me you were at the mall. You'll be home for dinner soon? I'm not there yet, but I have a lot of good stuff to tell everyone," my dad said in a chipper mood.

Struggling not to mess up his day, I barely breathed, "Daddy . . ."

"Yeah?"

"I'm scared."

"Of what? It doesn't matter what happens with the election, we gave our best go at it. You don't have to worry about whether I lose, or win for that matter. It's in God's hands."

"No, no, Daddy. Remember when I was in the pageant? The guy that you saw me with? You told me to not mess with him anymore? Well, I messed with him again."

"What are you talking about, Slade?"

"Well I mean . . . he owes these guys some

money, and I think he's in trouble. I'm on my way to this house with his mom and this cop and . . ."

"You're on your way where?" my dad yelled, not happy for sure. "Give me the address right now! And don't you even go in there, girl. You aren't anybody's private investigator."

"But he's my friend, Dad!"

"You don't need to go at all."

"Dad, you're just going to have to be angry with me because I'm going over there. I'm really, really worried about him."

"What if you get killed too?"

"Dad, just come. I'll text you the address," I said before hanging up.

My cell rang and rang. It was my father calling back. I knew I was going against his wishes, but I wanted him to know I didn't want him to stop me. I needed him to help. I texted him the address when I was at a stoplight, and then I proceeded to help my guy.

***

An hour and a half later, there was a major police operation going on at the house in question. Sam snooped around and found enough probable cause to get other officers out there. Drugs were being sold on the property, but Ms. Hardy was all stressed out because while the cops were bringing bad guys out, Avery was still nowhere to be found.

Boots was brought out in handcuffs, and she rushed up to him and started pounding on his chest.

"Where's my son? Where's my son? What have you done with my son?" she shouted.

Sam tried to pull her away.

"You got my money?" Boots rudely said to her.

"No!" she shouted, still distraught.

"Then I don't know what you're talking about."

And the police carried him away.

"Oh my gosh, Daddy, what if they killed him?" I said to my father, who wouldn't let me get anywhere near the house.

Suddenly, gunshots were fired inside the house. When someone within it yelled for the police to get back, my dad really became concerned and told me not to move. Then he rushed toward the back of the house.

I screamed out, "Daddy! Daddy!"

With the gunshots coming from the police outside and from someone else inside, I could only hope my dad didn't get mixed in the cross-fire. About fifteen minutes later, media trucks were surrounding us.

Sam yelled out, "Hold your fire! We're coming out. Call for an ambulance. We've got one badly wounded."

The moment was chaotic. My dad came out of the house with two other guys who dropped their guns as soon as they stepped outside. My dad brought them over to law enforcement.

A reporter rushed past me and stepped to my father. "Mr. Sharp, you're running for mayor, but we didn't know you spent any time with the police academy."

My dad, walking to me, uttered, "I haven't."

The reporter would not move out of his way. "What made you get in the middle of a gun shoot-out? What you did was really, really dangerous. Why would you do something so foolhardy?"

"Just didn't want any more young men losing their lives to gun violence. I asked them if I could talk to them. They said yes, and the rest is history."

"What would you have done if they would have shot you?"

"I guess I wouldn't be running for mayor," he joked. "But I believe in all the citizens of Charlotte, even the ones who have lost their way. I was here and had to help."

All the attention turned to Sam, who was carrying a badly beaten person in his arms. Blood was dripping profusely. From my distance, I couldn't tell if he was shot or if he was just plain beaten up. But whatever he was wearing, Ms. Hardy recognized it.

"My baby, my baby!" She pushed through the cops and ran toward her son.

"I need paramedics!" Sam called out.

The medics rushed to get Avery on a stretcher. My dad wasn't there to hold me back anymore, but I didn't want the cops to stop me either, so I ran to Avery. One of his eyes was completely shut. The other was barely open.

His face looked unrecognizable.

"I'm sorry, Mom. I'm sorry," he said in an altered voice that sounded painful.

His mother looked over at me and smiled. "If she wouldn't have told us where you were, Avery, they could have killed you."

Getting upset as he saw me so distraught, he said again, "I'm sorry. I'm sorry."

"It's okay, baby. It's okay," she said. I knew he was sorry I was brought back there for another horrific encounter.

I guess my face said it all. I was so devastated to see him that way. My eyes were puffy too, and I was crying.

"Slade . . ."

"Shh! Don't talk," I said to him.

"Thank you," he uttered, as a teardrop fell from his one opened eye.

My dad came near us, and I said, "Thank my dad."

Avery uttered, "Sir, I'm, I'm . . ."

My dad touched his shoulder to ease him from talking and said, "Young man, I don't know what you're mixed up in."

"I owed 'em, sir. Just wanted to catch 'em doing what they do. They . . . they caught me," Avery talked anyway, though he could barely get words out.

My father said, "Whatever you were trying to do might have seemed good in theory, but nothing is worth losing your life. You're too young to be caught up with these guys anyway. I hope you young people get it. There is just no get-rich-quick scheme."

CHAPTER SEVEN
SUPERSTAR

"Avery! It's you! Oh my gosh are you okay?" I said into the receiver the next day, happy that he dialed my phone.

"Yeah, I'm alright. I'm back home. Just had some stitches and and a lot of bruises. They didn't even keep me overnight at the hospital. I hope your dad is not too mad at me. He's really the hero."

"Yeah . . ." I said, proud of my father.

Candidate Stanley Sharp had been all over the news the last twenty-four hours. My dad's campaign manager was saying he was going to win for sure. Over the last three months, he was the big hit at three big news stations. In August, he revealed that unlike his opponent, he was going to work to rid the city of domestic violence. In September, he helped to reveal that at a foster care house, the person in charge was taking advantage of the kids in state care. Now, he helped bust a big drug house.

"I hope he does win. Mad respect for the man. He is fearless. I can't believe he got in there and helped me like that. I know you would have never forgiven me if something would have happened to your dad trying to save me," Avery said.

"Well, can you tell me why you did it? Why'd you go back there, and you didn't have his money? You know Boots is crazy."

"I know. I thought I could reason with him."

"No, Avery, that's not all. I don't know if you remember, but you mentioned some scheme, some plan, something you were trying to catch them in. Obviously, it had to do with the drugs. Why are you trying to be a hero?"

"Because, I got to get my momma out of this mess I got her in. Honestly, I thought if I had evidence on what he was doing, I could reason with him to give me more time."

"But you're going to pay him back with your voice. You won the contest for Mundy Records."

"No, I guess that's what made me all crazy. I thought I was going to get an advance, be able to pay Boots back, get him off of my back, but I got a call from the record label, and the owner man told me he might have to close his business."

"What?" I said, shocked. "Are you serious?"

"I wish I was joking. Just when I thought I was catching a break, stuff goes wrong. I won the big contest, now I have nothing," Avery uttered with real despair in his voice.

Actually, I remembered being in Mr. Mundy's office, and he was telling my father and me how tough times were for his business. But neither of us realized that he truly meant within the next week he was going to have to close his doors. My dad had to know. Maybe he could help.

"Why don't you get some rest?" I said to Avery, thinking I needed to take this info to my father who had a track record of fixing everything.

"Wait, I got all your messages about wanting to cut a demo."

"But you got to get well first," I told him, knowing that was most important.

"I need that loot that you were going pay me to do it. How about in the next couple of days, you and your girl get into the studio and we lay this track?"

"If you're up to it . . ."

Cutting me off and wanting to show he was tough, he said, "Y'all just practice. I'll be fine."

I wanted to tell him that if everything with Mundy Records didn't work out, then maybe I could sign him to Sharp Records, but I didn't want to insult him like that. He was talented, and my label was just starting.

Avery made me feel real good when out of the blue he said, "Who knows? Maybe you get distribution going, and you can make me one of your artists."

I just smiled through the phone. I was working to make sure my future records had a way to get in the hands of the consumers. Yeah, I could sell out of my trunk, but if I got distribution in stores, I'd be rolling.

"My mom thinks you're an angel," he said, extending the conversation.

"Really? I thought she hated me," I replied, thinking back on all our interactions.

"What? You think she feels you're a little nosy, stuck-up, rich girl?" he teased.

"That sounds more accurate."

"Well she ain't mad at you being nosy anymore. Come on, if it wouldn't have been for you, she wouldn't know where I was. Big thanks, Slade. Straight up, big thanks," he said, being really sweet before we hung up.

I was sitting in the living room waiting on my parents to come home. I needed to tell my dad what was going on with Mundy Records, but all of a sudden, Shelby and Ansli cornered me.

"Uh, you deserve a prize," my oldest sister said.

"What are you talking about?" I said to Shelby, unsure of how to take her probe.

"Out of all the stuff the two of us have been through recently, bringing a bunch of attention to this family, girl, you take the cake, dealing with drug dealers. What were you thinking?" Shelby asked as she hit me upside the head.

"You two ought to understand. This guy caught my eye and . . ."

Shelby cut me off and mocked, "Yeah, we understand. He pulled you into some of everything."

"Right," Ansli said as she threw a concerned glare my way.

"Just be careful, alright, Slade?" Shelby said to me. "If you hang with some of those people, you'll be rolling in the fast lane, and there's no way you can slow down."

I was irritated because my sisters were acting like I wanted to be down with drug dealers. They knew guys could drag you into more than you wanted to know about or be involved in. However, I just nodded, trying not to be so defensive.

When my parents came home, Shelby and Ansli went with Mom to get details about the galleria event they had attended. Shelby wanted to hear all about the fashion, and Ansli wanted to see the pictures and upload them onto social media sites.

I was happy for the alone time with my father so I could tell him what I knew. He seemed weird, though. I couldn't figure out what was up.

Soon as I went to speak, he said, "Slade, I need to talk to you."

"Yes, sir," I reluctantly said as I followed him to his office, getting the feeling that what he was about to say wasn't good.

When we got into his office, he got right to it. "I just want to tell you I don't expect you to be hanging out with that young man from yesterday anymore."

"But Dad . . ."

"Don't 'but Dad' me . . ."

"No, I need him to help me with my music," I passionately explained.

"Honey, when you were with his mom, he was apologizing to me for almost getting you raped. I don't even know if he knew what he was saying because he was beat up so bad, but the fact that he put you in harm's way, exposing you to those guys, means I got to cut it off. So I'm telling you now that I don't want you to have anything to do with him. Do you got it?" he pointed at me and sternly stated.

Angrily I gritted my teeth and said, "Yes, sir."

"And what did you want to see me about?"

"He was supposed to be getting a record deal from your friend Mr. Mundy."

"Well, good for him," my dad replied, clearly half caring.

I tugged on my dad's shoulder so he could reconsider. I uttered, "I'm saying he's not all bad."

Letting me know there was no negotiating, he said, "Okay, but you're not going to deal with him. I'm telling you. We just talked about that."

"I know, I'm just saying Mr. Mundy is having issues with his record label. I think he's going to have to shut it down."

"What? No!" my dad said, and he looked through his cell phone and dialed his friend.

They talked for a few minutes, and my dad

put him on a three-way call with his banker friend. It was amazing the connections my father had. Nothing was promised over the phone, but Mr. Mundy had a meeting the next day. I could overhear Mr. Mundy telling my dad how much he appreciated him hooking that up.

"Slade, you and your sisters are something fierce."

I left out of the office with my lips poked out, and he stopped me.

"Hey, don't get mad at me because I don't want my daughter connected to a loser. I'm just saying," my father said.

He might as well be saying my life was over. I had a connection to Avery. Some kind of way I was going to have to figure out how to keep it going.

***

"Slade, I'm just glad we're friends. I've needed a good girlfriend. So many people have wanted to be my friend because of what they thought I could do for them or what my dad could do to help them, with him being the superintendent and all. You understand all that with your dad being important, too. You don't want anything from me," Charlotte said and she looked down, probably thinking about how shady people can be.

"I want you and me to practice. How 'bout that?" I said to her, as I tried to lighten the mood.

Not that I didn't want to get deep and have a good close girlfriend either, but I wanted us to practice because we were finally going to be going into the studio to cut a song. Charlotte talked me into setting it up with Avery and going around my dad. We hoped maybe the great sound would change his mind. Though I wasn't comfortable with the sneak idea, I felt I had no choice. And when we stepped into the studio, I wanted us to be prepared. Time was money in the studio. Since it was my money we'd be spending, I wanted to make it count.

"We can practice in just a sec, but I'm serious," she said, a little melancholy.

I knew why she was serious. Charlotte had invited me to have dinner with her whole family after we finished practicing. In a way, I guarded my family, and I'm sure she did, too. I understood people wanting something from you because of your dad's status. Her dad was a superintendent, and I wasn't sure if my dad was going to be the mayor, but from the looks of things, he had a pretty good shot. With the election just a week away, maybe Charlotte could give me some advice.

"So, with your dad having an important job and all, when people approach you, how do you know they're sincere?" I asked.

"If I don't know them at all, then I'm real leery. If I do know them and they still want to talk to my dad or want me to relay a message to my father, then I just have to hear them out. I realize that I am in a strong position, having my dad's ear and all. He can't be everywhere at all times, and I see what's going on at school. His job is to work for the citizens of the city, and, for sure, that includes the students, especially since he is the superintendent. If I know something is not right and I can help someone with a good reason get access to my dad, then I feel I'm supposed to do that."

Just as Charlotte said that, it dawned on me. I needed to talk to her father. Maybe he was the key to helping Taylor's mom's music program not get cancelled. We practiced a little, and right before we were going to dinner, I turned to Charlotte and gave her an intense look.

I said, "Okay, I'm one of those people who need you to help me get to your father."

"Huh?" she replied, confused.

Getting worked up because I wanted her to know I was really her friend, I said, "I mean, I don't want you to think that I am here because I want to talk to your dad. I mean, it just came up and . . ."

"Okay, Slade, I know you. What's up? What's going on?"

I shared everything with her. She was so appalled imagining the faces of the little kids having nowhere to go after school that she grabbed my hand, dragged me to her father, and had me tell him everything. Her father took in everything I said and committed to helping figure it out.

What was so awesome was that the next day, her dad and her cutie pie younger brother, Paris, came with me to Taylor's mom's afterschool class. The little kids sang for the superintendent. After they sang, he talked to a couple of them.

One little girl named Scarlet said, "Mr. Tendent, I love being here after school. I'm smarter because I sing. I make better grades now. I'm real confident. Please don't take this away."

A little freckle-faced boy named Ben said, "My mommy don't live with us no more. I don't know where she is, and my dad's in jail. I live with Nana. She loves me in this program. She says I'm not bad anymore. Please don't take it away."

And then a little boy named T.K. said, "I used to get bad marks in school 'til I started seeing Ms. Dale after school. Now I make good grades. You take away the only thing I'm good at, then I'll go back to being dumb again."

"No, young man. You will stay smart. I'm going work it out some way," Charlotte's father declared, making the room erupt with delight.

"I promise the budget will be reworked to keep this program."

When he said that, all the little kids in the afterschool program—approximately fifteen—rushed up and hugged him really tight. Then, they surrounded me. I couldn't get out of the place. The kids wanted to play with me, and they thanked me with tickles. The superintendent shook my hand and thanked me for caring. Taylor's mom hugged me, and said I went above and beyond.

What really got to me was before I left, Taylor stopped me. "Everything I put you through . . . you still helping my mom like this makes you the best person I know. I was an idiot to throw our friendship away. Dayna and Caylen get so jealous sometimes. It's like they don't want us to hang out with anybody outside of our group. I let them get in my head, and I threw a good friendship out the window. Right now, I guess I'm just asking you to . . . I don't know . . . give me another chance."

"Hey, you guys hurt me," I said. Then I knew I did care for her boo, and she didn't know that. "But I'm not perfect either. I was fighting y'all too. I'm just glad it seems like it's going to work out. These kids deserve a program."

"And you deserve a big apology," Taylor said. "I'm trying to give one."

"You gave me one before. You weren't totally wrong about me liking your guy."

"Avery's reached out and shared how everything went down with y'all and that I lost him because of my own crazy actions way before he met you. The right one for me will come along. You told me that, and I need a friend like you in my life," she said as we hugged.

***

I was supposed to be headed to the studio with Charlotte, but it just didn't seem right because my father told me to stay away from Avery. I had to get him to change his mind. I just didn't feel like it would work out if I went around him. But as soon as I went to him to plead my case, he didn't give me a chance to speak because he needed my help with a campaign event.

"But, Dad, I need to talk to you."

"No, no, no. I'm rushing. I just need you to come and go with me," he said, giving me no choice.

In the limo, I couldn't even talk to him because he was on his phone. I dozed off. When he told me to wake up, I was shocked to see we were at the Renaissance Theater.

"What are we doing here, Dad?" I asked.

There were lots of cars there too, but my dad was rushed off by his campaign team. Avery's mom rushed up to my father and whisked him away. I could only make out a part of the conversation when she said, "Thank you for helping me save my theater." What was my dad up to? What was going on? Why were we here? Why were all these people here, and where was Avery?

"Hey, Ms. Sharp," someone touched me on the shoulder and said.

When I turned around, I was surprised to see Mr. Mundy. "Hey, sir."

"I got to tell you, you and Avery really pulled it off," he shared, letting me in on something I did not know.

Confused, I shook my head. I remember my dad was talking to him on the phone and put him in touch with the banker, but that was a week ago. What had happened since then? What did I miss?

Recognizing that I was dumbfounded, he explained, "I got a loan. My company isn't going under. I'm about to showcase Avery as a new artist along with my top selling group too."

"Smash Rose is going to perform?" I questioned, loving the cool, country-rock band whose songs had been climbing the charts.

"Yup."

"Have you seen Avery?" I asked.

"Yeah. He's around the corner in the dressing room."

"Okay, thank you."

I was just about to turn to go there when Mr. Mundy said, "One more thing. I want to talk to you about your record label."

"Well, I'm trying to start one," I said, knowing he didn't want to be bored with my lil' dreams.

"Well, I know I wasn't positive about it when

your dad first brought you to talk to me, but we have a couple of independent labels signed to Mundy to help with their distribution. If their label succeeds, my label does too. I'd love to sit down with you to talk about what you're doing and possibly get you a distribution deal."

"So you mean my record label could be under your label?"

"Yup. We could grow together."

"Wow! Can I run it by my parents?"

"Absolutely."

"So what's going on here?" I asked, still curious about why my dad brought me to the Renaissance.

"Your dad has brought a lot of influential folks in the city together tonight, not to give to his campaign, but to give to the arts. Tonight my artists are performing, and all the proceeds go to this theater."

"Well, if your artists are performing for free, how does that help?" I asked, really wanting to understand why he was so pumped about this.

"Great question, Slade. The publicity this charity event is generating will turn into big dollars. Sometimes you gotta give to get. Your dad his helping us all in this city to understand that concept, and Charlotte is going to be stronger because of his vision."

"Wow!" I said, completely blown away. I now understood why Avery's mom was so excited to see my father.

When Mr. Mundy went to go to take a seat, I sat on the stairs. The first time I was sitting there I was crying. I'd lost a pageant, and I thought my dreams were over. The second time I was there I was scared to death thinking Avery's life was over. Now, weeks later, I realized that no one controlled my dream but me. You've got to do things the right way so you won't be indebted to shady folks.

I'd started a record label, and, sure, we hadn't even cut our first demo, but the fact that I believed I could gave me all the confidence I needed to sit there for a second and reflect. I didn't want to get in my own way. I didn't want to do things that messed me up. I didn't want to bust into Avery's dressing room and take the kiss to the next level. My dad told me I couldn't see him, and even though he was here helping Avery's mom, that didn't mean all was good for Avery to be my boo.

"Going through your thoughts, pretty lady?" I heard Avery say.

His voice was just as husky and sexy as it was weeks ago when he encouraged me and dried my tears. I didn't want to look his way. The undeniable chemistry between us won out.

"I miss you," he said, smiling all wide.

"I'm just glad you're better," I told him, scared to say more.

"A few bumps and bruises can't keep a brother down. But I'm sorry I hadn't called. I've been busy with Mr. Mundy. Things worked out for his company. I'm going to have a single out."

"Yeah, he just told me. Can't wait to hear you perform on that stage."

"But you haven't been calling me either. Everything alright?"

Before I could answer "no," I heard my father's authoritative voice say, "Slade Sharp!"

"Dad, Dad, I was looking for you. I, I was

just sitting here, and Avery came over. It's not like we bumped into . . ."

"You don't have to explain," my father said, cutting me off. "Avery's cool." I looked really confused. "His mom, he and I have been talking over the last couple of days. I've actually been down in the studio with Mundy, and Avery's got talent like you said."

Could this be happening? When a tear welled up, I knew this was real. My dad was coming around.

My father leaned in and said, "I stand corrected. You don't need to get too turnt up with this guy, but I approve, baby."

I just hugged my dad so tight. I gave Avery a thumbs up. He winked.

"You gonna keep things on the up and up though, right, young man?" my father said to Avery. He noticed Avery checking me out. "We talked about guidelines with my daughter, and we also talked about you walking the right way."

"Yeah, I just got to get these guys their money back, sir. I owe three Gs," Avery admitted as his grin turned to worry.

"With them sitting in jail, they won't be coming looking for it no time soon. I'm sure you learned your lesson that you can't go to shady characters to right things wrong in your life." Avery nodded and my dad touched his shoulder. "You better get on out there. Show's ready to start."

My dad turned around and walked out. I couldn't believe he was so awesome. I'd seen Shelby and Ansli come to this big revelation that our father was the bomb over the past few months, and now it was my turn. Both of them were eighteen and could vote. Though I wasn't old enough to cast mine for Stanley Sharp, I sure wanted to. Not because Stanley Sharp was my father, but because he was a great man who had big visions and wanted to do all he could to help everybody win in Charlotte.

"I'll let you go get ready to perform," I said, turning away.

Avery gently grabbed my hand and said, "Nuh-uh, you're not getting away from me that fast."

Avery pulled me to him. He kissed me long,

but when the kiss was over, he didn't let go of my hand. He actually dragged me on stage with him.

I had no choice but to follow. Avery mouthed, "Trust me." When we got to the stage, the audience roared.

Avery commanded the mic like a pro and said, "Hey everybody, I'm Avery Hardy, and I'm excited to be the newest solo artist for Mundy Records. Thanks for coming out tonight for this great event. I want to sing my new single for you, but before I do that, I'd like to ask this lovely lady here if she would join me in a song we sang in the studio a couple weeks ago. I know this song needs to be on the album. You tell us if you agree."

When the music came on, I realized this was the song we made at Boots' house. The house lights dimmed, and the spotlight came on Avery and me. Our eyes connected, and our voices meshed. After hearing only the first few opening bars, the crowd went wild.

All was right with my world. My dad was so close to being the mayor. My family was great.

I'd always wanted friends outside of my sisters, and now I had two, Charlotte and Taylor. A month ago, I didn't think I was ready for a boyfriend, but I guess a boyfriend was ready for me. To make it all great, I got my dream. This time I wasn't asleep. I was fully awake, enjoying my reality. I was in my element, giving it my all and feeling like a superstar.

ACKNOWLEDGMENTS

Shout outs to all those who help me give it my all.

To my parents, Dr. Franklin and Shirley Perry, you are some turnt up parents who loved me with all you had.

To my Publisher, especially, production editor, Martha Kranes, you all are a turnt up company who prints works that make a difference.

To my extended family, you are my turnt up family that gives me wings to fly.

To my assistants Shaneen Clay, Alyxandra Pinkston, and Candace Johnson, you are some turnt up young ladies who help me write stories that matter.

To my dear friends, you are a group of turnt up real friends that I can't live without.

To my teens, Dustyn, Sydni, and Sheldyn, you are my turnt up babies who I work hard to help succeed.

To my husband, Derrick, you give me turnt up love that fills my heart.

To my readers, you are a turnt up crew and I'm proud of you doing more to become all you can be.

And to my Heavenly Father, you are my turnt up Savior and you bless me by giving my life purpose.

ABOUT THE AUTHOR

STEPHANIE PERRY MOORE is the author of more than sixty young adult titles, including the Grovehill Giants series, the Lockwood Lions series, Payton Skky series, the Laurel Shadrach series, the Perry Skky Jr. series, the Yasmin Peace series, the Faith Thomas Novelzine series, the Carmen Browne series, the Morgan Love series, the Alec London series, and the Beta Gamma Pi series. Mrs. Moore is a motivational speaker who enjoys encouraging young people to achieve every attainable dream. She lives in the greater Atlanta area with her husband, Derrick, and their three children. Visit her website at www.stephanieperrymoore.com.

THE **SHARP** SISTERS

Make Something of It
STEPHANIE PERRY MOORE

Better Than
Picture Perfect
STEPHANIE PERRY MOORE

Turn Up
for Real
STEPHANIE PERRY MOORE

Truth and
Nothing But
STEPHANIE PERRY MOORE

Icing on the Cake
STEPHANIE PERRY MOORE

SOUTHSIDE HIGH

ARE YOU A SURVIVOR?

CHECK OUT all the books in the

URVIVING SOUTH SIDE

collection

IT'S THE OPPORTUNITY OF A LIFETIME IF YOU CAN HANDLE IT.

Box-Office
Smash
D. M. PAIGE

≡OPPORTUNITY

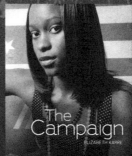

The
Campaign
ELIZABETH KARRE

≡OPPORTUNITY

Chart
Topper
D.M. PAIGE

≡OPPORTUNITY

The
Franchise
PATRICK JONES
with BRENT CHARTIER

≡OPPORTUNITY

Going to
Press
D.M. PAIGE

≡OPPORTUNITY

Size 0
D.M. PAIGE

≡OPPORTUNITY

≡OPPORTUNITY